man and beast

nathan hondros / damon lockwood

regime
books

Published by Regime Books in Australia 2009.
First Floor, 456 William Street, Perth
www.regimebooks.com.au

ISBN 978-0-646-51140-5

CONTENTS

Clifton Hill

1.

It is late morning and it is a beautiful clear day (I think today she will come). Everything is in its place and waits where it should be, satisfied. These warm drowsy mornings. I sometimes feel at these times I have shifted into an almost unreal place of delicate harmony until I realise it is the very actualness of these surroundings that make this feeling of contentment so precise. The quiet chrome of the kitchen sink is clean and clear, reflecting from within its grooves the late morning sun around the room. There is a pristine quality in the air, a clearing out of everything unnecessary except the reflected light that shines brightly into every corner of our apartment. From where I lie I can see a patch of pure blue sky through the window and the uppermost branches of a large eucalypt (our apartment is on the second or third floor). There is a gentle breeze today – the branches occasionally sway from side to side, touching both sides of the window before coming to rest in the centre again. I am also accompanied by the low soothing hum of the refrigerator and the occasional echo of distant traffic. On my left is the bathroom, smelling cool and clean with the promise of water (later in the day the sun will swing round and reflect a deep green light off the bathroom floor and walls into the rest of the apartment, a cooling light that calms the edges of all objects). The almost Zen-like architecture of synthesis in the room is complete and I am a willing part of it – there could be a terrible war raging not a hundred metres away and I would continue to wait here blissfully unaware.

When finally she does arrive it is early evening and the stronger colours of the day are receding from the room. In contrast she is bright and alive. She wears a tight red skirt that comes to just below her knees. The skirt is made of a thick stretchy material so as she moves about the apartment it follows the call of her arse then falls to the perfect line of her thigh. I begin already to feel sick in the pit of my stomach just watching her. She is wearing a black sleeveless blouse to match the precise cut of her black, bobbed

1

hair. When she entered the apartment I was desperate to take in everything, the smell of cigarettes, her dark sunglasses and disinterested air, the red and brown roofs glimpsed through the open doorway. She walks around the apartment distractedly for a little while not really acknowledging me, which I am used to – I know now I am really the only reason she comes here and I know that she knows that too. In the kitchen she pours herself a glass of water from the tap and then downs it in one long deep swig.

When she finally comes and sits next to me on the bed I am again engulfed with the complete smell of her perfume, perfume like sandalwood. Perhaps it is the smell of a moisturiser or maybe even just her natural smell I don't know, I entertain myself with these thoughts long after she has gone. I imagine this smell of hers rubs off on to anything she touches outside the apartment like a powder. I imagine a lot of things about her, I think of her often.

But now sitting on the bed right next to me she kicks off her shoes and moves to light another cigarette. The mattress ripples slightly underneath her. She lights her cigarette with a small blue zippo lighter then throws it away across the room. She looks down at me, and then notices my desperation, the strength of my erection. She runs the long red fingernail of her left index finger all up and along the left side of my body, all the way slowly from my knee to my armpit. Her nails are real and strong and she leaves a thin white graze mark all the way behind the path of her nail. She shifts her attention to my cock. Continuing to smoke and not altering her position on the bed at all she simply rubs the smooth ends of her fingers across the tip. I come stupidly and powerfully all over my pale stomach. She scoops the deposited strands up in her fingers and nails and drops them over my forehead and eyes. She is back and I am happy and she continues to smoke like a body made of embers.

Then after this gentle start we fuck all night, all night, stopping only occasionally for food and drink, rarely for respite. Tonight she has brought a mild chicken curry and for that I am very grateful. The food is only a small mercy in the greater ecstasy of the night though – tonight we do everything together, everything, any possible way we try. We screw all night and all over, armpits and breasts. We fuck until I am raw dear god, until she must be raw, until any pain rolls over and over itself and eats itself away. Left in the middle at the end are two wet creatures, one left breathing through the fanciful adorations of my love for her.

Her straight black hair rocks back and forth along the outside edges of her face. Her sleek inside thighs stiffen and release with the acoustic precision of music, the angles on her back tell stories and speak of their love for me. If ever I am in pain then the pain is real and I can hold her here with my eyes and my trust as she rides along screaming in the night air above me. If she tries to tear the ears off my head then this is good for I will grow them back again for her – I am safe at home when she is near.

2.

In the quiet morning she stands with her back to me, drinking coffee over the kitchen sink. She stands with her naked naked back to me and again now I know I am in love and in love with her again.

I would walk up behind her and enfold her in my arms before we float together and easily through the vast canyon of our dependency. I would stroke her hair and speak to her of mountains.

3.

In between times there is nothing, no desire or colour. In these endless troughs I sometimes think I am a figment of even my own imagination, or a punished constant dream for all the worst sinners in the world to visit during troubled sleep. In these times without her I discover it is possible for a human body to contain no experience, no name, a name denotes opinions, thoughts. I am a blind man only given sight when she is with me. I feel at times there is no synthesis of harmony or even awareness of physical surroundings, just a rambled despair that eats itself of purpose and space. I swallow again, one dry rasp closer to sight.

4.

Next time she comes I guess she has come straight from work – she looks very groomed and professional. There are no tight reds or short blacks today. Today she wears a dark grey skirt and jacket and underneath a dark blue blouse. Her dark sunglasses are replaced with a pair of thin framed reading glasses which I think really suit her. Like always though the whole outfit emphasises her perfectly conditioned body, eyes and cheekbones. She must be very popular at work. All the dickhead guys I imagine she works with must ache to have a piece of her. Too bad for them.

She comes in all agitated and abrupt, no hellos or greetings like she has some of the other times. She is through the front door and kicking off her shoes ripping off her earings moving towards the toilet, she may even be muttering beneath her breath. She doesn't look at me. She throws her grey handbag at me and moves away into the bathroom.

The handbag hits me clean on the torso. It flips over and scatters some of its contents over my chest and under my outstretched arms. One of these items is her purse, fallen open and exposed standing erect on my chest, revealing a pocket holding her drivers license... ...and, a name...

Finally.

In the next room the toilet flushes. In a moment she comes into the main space drying her hands and upon seeing me in an instant I think realises everything. She stops.

I have to reassure her, let her know that this is the best of all possible outcomes and that she has not in any way anything to fear, that this in fact is a moment of great celebration. I indicate with my head and my eyes that I want her to take my gag off. She seems distant and upset but begins to move closer. She gives me the signal that I mustn't shout or yell or I know what will happen. Of course yes, I nod, yes of course. She reaches down slow and deliberate and carefully pulls the old cloth over and off my head.

Melinda, I say, breathless, breathing too much and too often, Melinda Weeks, 24 Ashcroft Grove, Sunshine.

Something about her reduces, face and shoulders droop. So, she says.

This, I,... I laugh through a dry mouth for the sheer enormity of it – my greatest wish!

... it's over, she says.

No, what? I say, not hearing, this means I can come for you, when all this is over, I can come for you and find you and...

Yes, she says, exactly. For a moment she looks down at her hands and then moves off towards the kitchen.

Now the time has finally come I don't know what to say. And then we can be together, I say, really together...

Yes, she says from the kitchen, around the corner out of view.

I don't think I am even really talking to her or that she is listening to me but it doesn't matter. It's worked, Melinda, I say (I know her name!), it's really worked, you don't have to be scared of me any more like you were maybe at the start or like I was when we didn't really know each other at the start.

Yes, she says, walking towards me with a drink in her hand.

Now I know your name I can always find you and then make you happy and do what you want me to do, I feel weak at the thought of it.

Yes, she says, sitting on the bed beside me. Drink this to celebrate hey? she says, offering me the drink. I lift my mouth and she helps with a hand at the back of my head, my arms still straight out from me and tied somewhere beneath the bed, just like my feet. Not that any of that really matters any more. I lift my head and take a good long drink. Whisky! She must be as happy and as excited as I am. I thrash about on the bed like a little boy before Christmas.

Do you know what this means, do you know what this really means? I say. She sits on the bed looking down at me. She nods her pretty head very slowly. But this is great, I say, getting lost in the possibilities, this is the best thing that could have ever happened.

I am almost delirious with the implications of such a chance event finally delivering to me this woman's name who for as long as I can remember now has been my whole and total world, in fact I start to feel quite light headed. I think I was getting a little bit too excited for my weakened but overjoyed state. The walls begin to blur and the ceiling swim a little. Maybe my body rises and then becomes very heavy. Rolling around in the mix I think I imagine almost her eyes beginning to water, but then she falls away in the dark and my bed, and, shoulders

I become aware of my limbs and my joints aching and then coming up through the darker layers I am awake and aware of the room. Everything is very, very clean. The carpet is clear and sparse, cupboards and windows appear fresh and stripped back upon themselves a layer. My sheets are changed and there is the very thick bite of a strong disinfectant in the air.

She is just leaving through the front door with a plastic bag of rubbish and other stuff, bottles and plates and green rubber gloves. My gag is back on and tightened. The straps around my legs and my arms have been changed and tightened. She sees me stir on the bed, watches me watching her. She waves lightly back to me like a new aquaitence popping off home after a short visit. She has a set of keys in her mouth and she has brushed her hair straight and flat.

She moves out and closes the door behind her and the apartment is clean and quiet and then very empty. It seems I may have known she was about to leave because as soon as she does my head becomes weighed down again and I sink back to the mattress waiting already until the next time she comes with the stories of her skin and the flesh of her thighs.

5.

but then of course at these times there is no need for a panic, she is busy like her and elsewhere and every moment closer for the longer she stays away the sooner she will be here…but even to myself these colours sometimes are engulfing, bright like a screen or shifting into a pure clear blanket of white there is a smell that remains and plays around my face like fingers, like vanilla sometimes then other times waste like shit or like Wednesday I came up a while later, some time after I had seen her leave with her keys in her mouth and with the bag of rubbish and stuff new supplies   I just can't leave this bed off my skin, around like worms, just eat my stomach and then okay, eat my stomach and my fist and swallow my eyes and ceiling and then fine and if the blue square strikes I could dodge it maybe and move But patience, for she is not far away with a fist love like my itching back and knowing curve warmed hand around my face, deep falling over each other down sand dunes and skies shining arms and bones but this hair in my, mouth and this tired,

    tired

Faultlines

Disappearing seemed easy after I managed it. There was a form for it, like everything else; required, signed and submitted. Then a bureaucrat posts out a slip proving your leave has been approved. Then when those days come, those white undulating hours, there is nothing left but to get in the car and drive; not to the hospital like any other day, but south. Along the ocean road, past the last suburb, through the scrub, out into the bush. Out, down, away. Forced along, almost absent of yourself, for miles until you come across the house you've rented, that was built lifetimes ago between the vineyard and the lake.

But also you can still hear the thrumming of the old world you've left, for somewhere far away the hospital is ticking over.

July had been soaked and cold, but we left in its last week, hoping for a thriving fireplace and more red wine than we could drink. For a few hours I couldn't relax. I unpacked and inspected the rooms. I tried to read but couldn't sit in the burgundy velvety chair for long enough. I thought, by now I'd be filling the resident's list, by now I'd be rushing to the outpatients clinic, by now I'd try and get down a coffee. By now, maybe, the nurse wrapped confidentially in tight white cotton that I stared at sometimes would be passing me on her way on to the afternoon shift.

How many days can it take before the skin is free of hospital light, before I can close my eyes without seeing the amorphous faces of patient after patient, et cetera, and so on. The fresh water teemed at the edge of the lake and we caught more than we could eat with an old net. How many days down here before I can sleep without hearing in my thickening mind the whir of fluorescent lights.

She knew I was on edge, still blistering from work. I scraped off the gas barbecue and cooked the fish out on the porch in the raw wind, then watched as she made the salad with her hands that looked too cold because she had been running them under water. I didn't know what to say, because I knew I couldn't say anything about work, which was everything I knew at that moment.

She didn't even look at me while we ate.

'I'm glad we're here,' was all I could think up eventually and it was a lie. She smiled, but still looked down at her plate.

Moving her food around on its ceramic surface. This fish has too little flesh, I thought. I waited for her to speak, but she didn't, although a tranquil look had set over her eyes and mouth, as though I had annoyed her in some vague way and she was showing me that I had been overcome. The kitchen had too much wood panelling and the table where we sat was laminated. We looked through dark windows over the vineyard we could now only see in the yellow light of a the bare bulb that kept away mosquitoes.

'What colour is the word "doctor"?' I asked her. She saw words as colours (colour synesthesia), and looked up at me, knowing I had found a way to talk about work without talking about work.

She tilted her head on the side and said, 'It doesn't have a colour.'

'But everything has a colour,' I said. That's what I thought.

'The "d" is brown, but the "o" is white. So the whole thing doesn't have a colour.'

In the hospital nothing has colour. I thought about the walls, but everything, everything was white or types of black, especially blood, which I never remember as red, only black, sometimes purple black, perhaps, but somehow beyond colour. Even the hair tied up delicately behind the heads of nurses was bound to be white or black. As I remembered it. I'd thought that Gia always had a colour for a word.

'Does "hospital" have a colour?' I asked.

'Brown. Maybe beige,' said Gia.

'Probably about right,' I said. 'Though I see black and white.'

'You can't think about work all week. How am I supposed to relax with you so wound up?' She knew I was trying, but your mind wanders through all that it knows best of all: the bodies and prescriptions for bodies. Words you say over the dying which are the new last rites, the doctor's last morphine injection, to sleep perchance to dream.

C'mon, I thought, think of her. The way you love the shape of her face and the blush she no longer needs to wear because her cheeks are pink enough. Think of her body, alive and still firm, tightening with hunger for all those years we let go between ourselves, but which can now be arrested this week, if we stop to think about it. I've missed you every day the hospital took me away. But here again I thought of the hospital.

'What colour is "waiting"?'

'Definitely purple. "W" is always purple.'

We carried the plates to the sink and I thought about all these moments I was so close to her. I put my arms around her as she filled the sink with hot water.

'You're hopeless,' she said. I was tense. It was all still with me. 'Go for a walk and relax. Don't come back until its out of your system.'

She knew me best. Outside the vineyard was dark. I wanted the cold soil under my naked feet. I thought, how much I'd love to stumble through it alone, reaching through vine leaves in the dark, finding my way. There is a clarity about night away from the city, an ease with which light transpires across the road and the vines, so it vaguely pushes into the scrub. From the house I followed the path to the footbridge that crossed the narrowing of the lake and from there walked into the vineyard. Off in the middle distance, a window was lit in the second house on the property, which, the caretaker had told me, was rented to a restauranteur. What colour would Gia make of that word? I guessed red. Obviously.

What a strange life, I thought. To own a restaurant. The kitchen's steam, the calm rush of waiters. Occasionally, as with all of us, I speculated on the jobs I could never hold. There are those who imagine themselves as doctors, poor souls. Like I was once. A child, poor boy, imagining the Latin names of my own anatomy, running my fingers over old diagrams of nerves and cells. Thinking of words as seductive as physiology and endocrinology as though they were the surface of a foreign world.

I'd seen the restauranteur stalking around the garden that bordered his rented house, his face flushed and his long thin legs sterile as they came out of his shorts. And his gut. Not severe, but obvious because of his old spindly limbs.

He'd looked up and nodded at me, his face unchanged. His eyes were fiercely narrow.

Between the two great vines where I stood I sensed the soft earth beneath my feet. I came to a fence and followed it down an incline where my own rented house couldn't be seen behind a row of old trees. Instead, I watched the restauranteur's house, the lit window. I followed the fenceline down until I could see through it.

Out here, I am invisible, I thought. Shrouded in the scrub. Black against black outside a window that couldn't be seen through.

The restauranteur sat in a cane chair with an open newspaper in his fingers. A woman stood in front of a mirror I couldn't see all of and combed out her dark hair. She turned to look at the restauranteur when he rustled the pages of his newspaper.

She combed out her hair and I looked between her naked back and the restauranteur's narrow eyes absorbed as they were in the newsprint. Turning to him, she placed her hands on her hips and spoke. He shook his head without looking at her. While she faced him, I saw the profile of her breasts, capped off by erect flesh the colour of bread. I wanted to shout to her, 'yes,' in answer to whatever question it was that made him shake to head; yes, a thousand times, yes. She put the comb up to her hair again, turning back to the mirror. Then it overcame me, the rushing blood, a sudden lightness.

The nauseous pressure of blood, the spinning of the head. More than anything I wanted her as she formed herself in the room's sub-light, betraying the lover with her existent skin, this man who couldn't even see her as he folded his paper and left the room. As he left the room, I saw him swallowed by gloom, disappearing. He would never return, I imagined, as the shade of the doorway carried him off.

The woman put her hairbrush down and turned towards the window where I watched her breasts. Am I once again an adolescent? I asked myself. A pervert, at this age? Walk away, I thought. But she unbuckled her belt and dropped her jeans, then her knickers. I caught a glimpse of the darkness of her as he returned to the room and she lay down on a bed where I couldn't see her. Without deciding to, almost as a reflex, I bent down and felt the earth around my feet until I clutched a stone, which I threw at the window. What for? It struck the glass but didn't break it. The restauranteur looked up and walked to the window, pressing his face against the glass and holding his hand against his forehead, so that he could see outside.

Could he see me? I felt as though he was staring at me, but I couldn't move. Her head appeared for a moment just inside the window frame.

Then another impulse beyond my control; I lay on the cold wet ground and looked up at the clear ink blue black sky. Moisture seeped through my clothes and a biting cold encased my shoulders. Beneath me a faultline opened. A gaping wound that consumed me. A blanket of cold wet ground. Then the hospital was almost gone, along with me, into the schism. Everything I was at that moment penetrated the image I carried of a woman brushing out her hair, the room around her subsumed in pale light. Come on, I'd call to her, come out in the open, away from him. He'll never see you the way I can.

When I stood, I saw they'd turned out the light.

Thank God, I thought. Nothing around me seemed real, not even the clarity through which I saw the lights of our rented house, the reflection off the car, scattered chairs in the gaseous yellow light. Unreal and far away.

I had crept back to the house, caked in wet dirt and rotten grapes. Gia lay on the bed, which I knelt beside. I kissed her on the mouth and was glad about the heavy lipstick that she hadn't yet wiped off. The line of her body in the lamplight was remorseless as she rolled on to her side. Here is my lost love, I thought, the shapes women make, the luniform digressions of a naked back. It soaked into me as though I was blotting paper. As she fell asleep I knelt beside her, resting my head on the blanket that I'd pulled up over her.

'Gia?' I asked.

'Mmmm?' But she was asleep. I put my nose in her hair to smell it, but it smelled of barbecue smoke.

How was my mind so frail and petrified? I knelt beside her for a while, perched above all I could think, outside of myself, not thinking much at all. I wished she was awake, so I could put my mouth over her, climb over her and fuck away this residue, the incomplete assurance I tried to give myself. It is only work, but family is vital; lose it all and walk away? How is losing so difficult? The clock seemed so loud, coming as it was from another room.

'What am I going to do?' I asked her sleeping form, and for a moment, she stirred. Then went on sleeping.

I climb in beside her.

What else would I dream about that night but the hospital? But also the restauranteur and his mistress, his skinny limbs protruding out of the hospital sheets, her back to me as I stood in the doorway, her hands and fingers combing out her hair. Was he dead? I couldn't see, but her shoulders quivered as though she was crying.

'What's wrong?' I asked her, but she still faced away from me. I moved closer to the restauranteur and saw that his chest still heaved. I wanted to tell her that he was still alive, to shake her by the shoulders and say, do you see? The dead ones have an inertia that is overwhelming; I once told an intern that the dead are stiller than stones. Beneath the skin and hair and eyelids of the living you can see all the potential energy, ready to spring out in spectacular form and motion.

But I looked again and, of course, he was dead. That's the inevitable direction of the imagination. Perverse motionlessness. She ran her fingers through her hair, and I faced her back. What could I have said? His body was watercolour blue.

I had woken just before Gia stirred, thinking about the hospital. Then she rolled towards me and opened her eyes.

'What colour is "synesthesia"?' I asked her.

'Definitely red.' Her eyes narrowed.

'I dreamed I saw the restauranteur from the other house die,' I said. 'Just a strange dream.'

'A hospital dream?' she asked.

'That's where they were,' I said. 'What colour is "cadaver"?'

And she sighed. 'Pale blue.'

Why had the earth opened like a gaping mouth and swallowed part of me? But, I thought, there is no open mouth beneath me, no open ground, just a warm white sheet and a hard bed. I thought about this for a moment. Had the faultline opened through me, dividing me in parts. The world outside my eyes seemed transformed, even though it was light and the room filled with green luminescence from the sun filtering through the drawn curtains.

There was another question I had. Gia put her hand to my forehead, where I was forced to notice it. She ran it through the hair on my temples to the back of my head, slowly moving her fingers across my scalp. She was half asleep. As she woke fully, an austerity settled into her features, a hardening of her eyes, a tautness in her pressing lips.

'I have one more,' I said, and she sighed once again. 'What colour is "faultline"?'

'"Faultline" is pink,' she said.

'Pink?' I was disappointed.

'Definitely pink. But a very pale pink. Fading into white, almost streaked. Almost white, maybe, but pink. Barely pink.'

And then I saw the word how she saw it; unfocussed; fading, then transparent; a tone just above the whitewashed pigments of the hospital walls.

Fallen Leaves

Colours fell around her like shades of tides, unclear patterns marking traces against the outline of the sky. The mid morning breeze, which was always at its strongest here, the town on the border, blew the fallen and falling leaves in panicked gusts and sweeping runs along the bitumen of the roads, passengers out of control on a helpless ride. Departed elm leaves gathered at her feet and around her stick, cast a frenzied look in her direction, then blew away and down the street, angling off curbs and in between the manic flock of each other. Autumn had come early this year… or maybe not, Mrs Winters had become unsure of time, especially in this last week, when all matter or consciousness had become more like imagined burns at the end of fingertips in the initial awakenings of a troubled sleep…

She was glad to be alone. Finally. The relentless procession of well-wishers, hangers on and Christians had started to become more than a nuisance; a trial, especially the Christians. Just because she and Mr Winters had continued the tradition of a Sunday appearance that had been written into the notepads of their minds by parents and predecessors somehow managed to result in the visitation of a whole section of people who had always apparently cared. She was glad her silence was taken as mourning – surely most of the people who had held her hand over the past week would have been disturbed to discover her inner thoughts were more geared towards confusion at their appearance and boredom of repetition than at despair of her loss. The condensation of brewed tea and buttered buns now filled every room of her house.

She had always liked the autumn. It was always a tenuous balance between melancholy and inspiration. She had now seen many autumns, seventy-two, this her seventy third. No matter how many years passed she was always reminded on those first few days of the numerous local trees shedding their leaves and creating a rain of ash, of early times, much earlier times, playing in the playground, swinging from the beams in a thin yellow cotton dress with similar bright faced girls whose names had long since left her until the sun went behind the mountains and the silver hand of early night began to find its way between the trunks of the trees and the naked steel of the playground equipment. Many more seasons had washed over her but always for a time in early autumn she was released from the disorientations of experience and relived a life that was simply unencumbered by anything. She wondered how many more she would see, this now being her first alone for some time. She caught a shrill breath of cold in her lungs, stumbled over the pavement, her walking stick finding the way between the cracks and mounds of concrete.

Mrs Winters was heading towards the storm water drains down Amherst Street. She was wrapped in a grey woollen cardigan and a multi-coloured scarf a silent but interested niece had made for her. Cars passed in some sense of direction though for her they meant nothing, faceless vehicles on a supposed mission of living. She didn't expect to find anything new at the drains, nothing emotionally, but she was prepared for all eventualities. Life could turn in an instant, often for the worst, sometimes for the best, always for the uninitiated. How else could she explain still living in the town she had lived in all her life, guessing at designs, unsure of history, past or future? She passed houses she had lived near all her life and couldn't remember one particular feature about any of them.

She wondered what she had been wearing last time she was here, last Tuesday, a departing day in the shadows of late afternoon. Was it exactly the same? Maurie had been dressed in nothing spectacular, even for this undeniable occasion – he had always been that way, and she had loved him fully because of it. Brown slacks with ironed lines down the legs and a thin cotton shirt rucked over the now prominent drop of his back. He would be cold before the end. Mrs Winters remembers a green about her, a cardigan? Or simple sweater. She doubts she would ever remember completely, her mental state had been in such an alternate land they could have been dressed in reflective suits and still she would imagine her recollections would be the same, and as blurred. All she remembered was that it had been a little bit warmer that day, and less disruptive. In all ways intentions had been clearer.

For a moment she thought of the empty bed waiting for her at home tonight, the familiar indentations on one side now left to their own resurrections. She stumbled on a little quicker, aware of the rustling sounded by the dead leaves around her.

Maurie had been sick for a little while, but not too much sicker than her, both showing the failings of a life lived and challenges endured. His crones disease had made him less determined than her, and yet still she had not really conceived the possibility of finality, and certainly not of separation. She still felt that morning clearly, sun reflecting off the sink, warm suds and pieces of soggy food surrounding her hands, when, as had been the inclination that had grown over their fifty one years of togetherness, she felt him slowly approach from behind. Who could tell if the morning had suddenly hushed itself, that for a time all revolutions had slowed, or that in reflection the moment had resigned itself to a stilled photograph. She ceased her hands in the water, he placed his left hand on her shoulder, and she turned. Mrs Winters saw a clearness in her partners' eyes that was bereft of judgement or decision, just a culmination of interspersed seconds that could suggest the relevance of a person's existence. He kept his hand on her shoulder, unblinking, and told her, 'I know exactly when I am going to die.'

The odd thing was they neither of them questioned it. She remembers them soon afterwards sitting in silence at the kitchen table, holding hands, watching over a layer just above the table cloth. Mrs Winters knew her husband would tell her when he was going to die so she had no need to ask. She knew he would tell her soon. The afternoon drifted into something other than silence, a waking dream, an unreality of anything solid or furniture.

It began to rain incredibly hard that night, torrents of unrelenting rain speared directly and continuously towards the ground. They held each other then, frail yet complete, total in each others arms listening to the downpour outside. They sometimes whispered small things in the others ears, that is how close they were, not even the fury outside and the beating wind could deafen the reassurances of love, the reminiscences of a life shared and adorations realised filtering down with a soft breath into their partners souls. Two weeks ago to the day Mr and Mrs Winters held each other in their much used and understood bed and taught their partner about love. Two weeks ago my life was very different, thought Mrs Winters. She said it out loud.

'Two weeks ago my life was very different.'

Nobody heard.

She remembered Maurie almost fell on this corner she was now turning, a raised uneven part of the ground. He had stumbled and almost fallen, steadied himself by himself and on the balance of his wife's arm. Careful, she said, you might fall and hurt yourself. They had stopped, looked at their open faces, and broken into laughter, leaning on each others laughter. Here, with twenty minutes of his life remaining, she was still concerned about him falling and hurting himself. To laugh at this time was a relief, an unexpected lump right at the very end. Turning the corner now she felt something swell inside her, a pulse, a fist maybe, adorned with either thorns or release. She pushed it away, anyway. She wanted nothing to hold at the moment.

It had rained for the rest of the week after Maurie's announcement. She herself was almost unaware of it – if it had to be this way then this is the way it had to be. Maurie confirmed this on an unusually dark afternoon around four o'clock when she found him staring into their backyard from the lounge room. He held his hands behind his back and looked out upon the deluge, the clogs and clumps of rain drenched leaves and upturned soil. She had moved up to him and held him. This is what I expected, he said, this makes sense. Which, considering the circumstances, was almost the most ridiculous thing he could say. She understood, though, understood for a moment the relentless nature of time, the pointless exercise of question.

The rain had turned the storm water drains into a thoroughfare, an unceasing tirade of flotsam and shopping trolleys and plastic bags. The push had eased slightly on the last morning the old couple, talking with the larger brains of their body, listening to each other's rhythms, had closed and locked their front door, the unusual habit of Mr Winters twisting the knob three times to make sure the door was good and locked. He caught himself just at the end of his ritual, wondering for a moment what it matters for this time. There was still his wife, he decided – does she remain my wife after I die? He veered away from the door, glad to notice his wife seemed preoccupied with the irrelevant machinations of their street when he turned around.

Mrs Winters wasn't overly pleased with her husband's final decision, or the decision that had been made for him, as he said. Of course the storm water drains were dangerous, not for an empty shell though, as he argued. He had never had any special connection to the place though, neither of them had. All he knew was that he had seen himself dying beside it, and it was irreversible, irreplaceable. She had supported him through everything, and he her – was she to change that now? The afternoon had finally sank upon them like a dusk, hobbling up to a place where the banks of the drains were at their slightest, and the descent the easiest.

What had she expected? A heart attack can be a guillotine, turning men's faces blue and collapsing a chest. Maurie's had come slowly (she suspected he controlled it for her sake, thinking of her even under the wide hand of death) – his breath shortened, his eyes widened and his lips grew dry and grey. They had been lying on the bank of the drain, Maurie's feet already placed in the running, dirty water. Mrs Winters couldn't remember if there had been great words of departure, his sweet head resting on the curve of her shoulder and her hand on his lessening heart had probably spoken a thousand more worlds than words ever could. He slipped away finally, his grip on her hand her life reducing, the strands of their life together evaporating like one single morning of dew drying away in the sun. She followed his demands as she said she would – it was at least the last thing she could do for this man she had loved. Feeling as empty as her recently departed husband, she stood out from under him, careful but unable to steady his lolling head, and moved him around and into the running passages of the constant storm drain waters. The rapids carried him away, undercurrents sometimes pulling the upper part of his torso through and under the collected flotsam that he was now a part of, sometimes allowing his face to edge above the grey water. He disappeared from view relatively quickly, and she was left alone, standing alone on the littered embankment, unsure of what to do with hands she had owned all her life, listening to the fog increasing in her mind.

She had not been home long before they came, two of them, an old rotund man and a young female officer with short blonde hair whose concerned face would have told her everything if she didn't already know. She's going to have to get better at this, Mrs Winters had thought. Perhaps she could learn from the older, larger policeman, who, with hat respectfully held in his large stubby fingers, calmly told her that her husband was dead, recently dead, and after a massive stroke had unfortunately fallen and been washed away down the storm drains. The young officer's eyes swelled with water themselves, translating the old woman's pain on to her self.

Mrs Winters had not expected the visit to cause her any unexpected misery or shock, she was concerned her part in his end would be exposed, unable to display the expected signs of loss, but in a simple moment, and for the first time she had thought of it, she had asked, more to herself than the sympathetic policemen, 'But why the storm water drains?' Her frail, suddenly frailer body had shook with released tears at the sadness of it all, the ridiculousness of it all, the undeniable tide of time that turns all things into decay and erases even the memory of trees…

The afternoon was becoming increasingly cold. The old woman walking past the storm water drains was seen to pull her cardigan closer around her and seemed to keep her eyes averted from the now departing waters in the concrete lane ways. Suddenly she stopped, turned around and walked back the way she had been coming.

There was nothing to see here, Mrs Winters realised, no answers. The past was like the future only more definite and confusing. The constant parade of foliage continued around the corners of Mrs Winter's vision, falling paintings on a transparent canvas. She really did like the autumn, Mrs Winters decided, the refuse of leaves and the bustling sky – she had known autumn and would continue to do so, with or without her limbs.

She turned the corner that took her back to their house, and wondered for a moment if she had forgotten her keys.

Man to his Dog

I was there, outside the railway station. We could've always been there, just like the dirty bronze statues that ruin the *Jardin Goudouli*: they'd call us *Man with Dog* because you and I owned the place. And because of course that's exactly what we were.

For a few hours I leaned against the railings, you at my feet, a thousand men and women spilling from the doors of the station, every face warping to meet the brisk air. We alone knew exactly how light could be a blunt bastard in Toulouse when the cold sets in and you get lost in it all; the streets that lead to the station, the metro and its sewers, the narrow winding stairs. The sun won't warm us, but that afternoon I didn't care. Not for a while.

I was watching a woman in a black coat waiting to be collected when I noticed Adeline, who back then looked only vaguely familiar in her red cap. I saw she was walking into the city, away from the Gare Toulouse-Matabiau, towards Capital Square. It was Saturday, the markets were open, and the crowds came and went. I was getting colder then, but I didn't worry about you, you don't fucking care about anything. Soon I'll find somewhere to wash you in the river, but it didn't cross my mind that day. We were following her and everything about me was converging on that. She was older than me, older than I'd have preferred. She could've been one of us, though, in her dirty coat and old pants. Perhaps that's why I followed her. Her disarranged hair was tied up under her hat and the back of her neck was the colour of bread. She didn't look as though she was headed anywhere in particular.

She glanced over her shoulder at us, then found a seat in the park, near the last tree that was about to lose its foliage. Perhaps she had noticed that we had followed her. She was in the shade. I stood and watched her. She kept looking over and after a while, I went over and sat right next to her, so close I could see it made her uncomfortable. Her body stiffened and she lent back and away from me.

'You're looking at me too much,' she said, and looked at you, the dog. *Man with dog*. You have to remember her in those first few moments to understand any of this. 'Don't look at me so much.'

'I can look wherever I want,' I said, scratching you behind the ears. 'What's your name, if you have one?'

'Adeline,' she said. 'Before you say anything, I think it's strange. Don't know why it's my name, it just is.' I thought that she may have been too old for me, but she looked at me as though I was the very first thing she'd ever seen and after my fingers found their way into her, they came out like they were on fire.

'Adeline,' I said. 'I don't know about that name. Made it up, didn't you?' She put her hand on your head, which you didn't mind. Something in her was burning her up, you could tell from the way she looked at me. I gave her some wine (stolen) and we walked back to the station. I let her follow close, her hand hooked into my belt, although it was me that could barely stand, me who stumbled when she came up behind and stood on my heels as I tried to walk.

There are things I must have said to her that afternoon that I can't remember. I can't remember everything that happened before my hands found their way around her.

'You look like someone famous,' she said.

'Who, then?'

'I don't know. Someone who could be famous. Not someone who is. You have that look about you. Some people have that look, don't you think?'

I knew what she meant. 'You must be as mad as me,' I said. We said nothing for a while, but watched the people moving past, carrying bags, talking on cell phones with voices that were no longer connected to their bodies. It made her sad to watch. I could sense it about her.

Then it was dark and we were alone for a long time. Somehow I got closer to her and began feeling her beneath her slack clothes. She breathed at me, the tobacco on her mouth, the words she said that I couldn't understand, but which sounded like a rumbling in the guts; it came from somewhere in her throat though, as though she was trying to speak.

Then she said something like, 'You know how to touch me.' I didn't really; I touched her like I touched any other woman, my hand rubbing away at her loosening flesh. She groaned as she came and I filled myself with the smell of her perspiration, the dampness spreading out across the tops of her thighs. She said my name I think, but I said nothing, not even 'Adeline' or 'fuck' or 'god'; although all these things occurred to me. I didn't breathe, just so that I could take in the shuddering of her body.

'I'll leave you, you know' she said.

Even now I get light-headed when I think too much about her, just because of those few moments. There's not so much to us after all, not more than an hour or two that really matter in the end.

She breathed heavily for a few minutes. 'Couldn't get enough of that,' she said eventually. 'Where've you been all this time?'

She opened her mouth and kissed me as she finished speaking. There was not a hair's breadth between us, as though she wanted to get inside me. Adeline, I thought, I've been nowhere at all until now. I had a few euros, so we caught the train to Montpellier, but didn't go far from the station. I bought her a bottle of wine and held on to her hand while she drank it. I hadn't even fed you, which is something that I regret now that I think about it. I should always feed the dog first, shouldn't I, before looking after any woman, even her.

'Where are you going?' I said as she picked herself up off me. Where the fuck was she going now. I tried to hold her hand some more, but she was moving away, half turned towards me, with a look that wasn't confused, but resigned to something else. She shook her head with her face down, letting her hat conceal her eyes as she went.

'I'll go with you,' I said. Is that what she wanted? I shouted, 'Is that what you want?'

She left a burnt out cigarette beside me. 'I'll find you later, Adeline,' I called out. She heard me alright because she stopped just for a moment, before carrying on. She had disappeared into the background, so I didn't look for her anymore.

Then the anger came over me. When I found out she'd been followed about by Mattias. That fucking immigrant that I barely knew, who'd brought that bastard dog out on the street and made a fool of himself everywhere he went? With Adeline, I was shaken. I'd been inside her and thought about it all night and for days. Mattias was a shit, worse than the worst of us, slower, with a look in his eyes like he could see the coin he was about to lift out of your pocket. I'd watch him as he spoke, leaning against the rail, that dog of his unleashed, exhausted from hunger, and resting on a blanket in front of him. Adeline must have known him then, but later I saw them together behind the carpark of the station, dirty hands all over each other. Adeline, what was it? There was something that flared up for a moment with her. Something I couldn't hold in my hands.

Mattias, *vous con*, how I wished you were dead, sprawled out with the blood running out your fucking eyes. Is that what I wanted? When I saw them together, all I wanted was to be him, to be standing next to Adeline, getting the smell of her on my fingers again. I would have killed him just to stand in his place, where I was ten feet tall just a few days before. Up so close to that woman I wasn't really me anymore.

I saw him alone, smoking a cigarette outside the opera house, watching the crowds flow down to the Christmas markets; all the women in dark clothes trying not to look at him because he looked insane, avoiding the sharp corners of his scowl.

'Mattias,' I said to him, 'I'll break your skull open. It would be right, if I

did. I saw you with Adeline.' I paused, and he said nothing. 'She's mine.'
    'Who?'
    'You fucking well know.'
    'Whoever she is, she's no one's,' he said.
    'I'm the saddest bastard alive, aren't I, wishing I was you?'
    I walked away, feeling as though I should have torn him apart. I could of. He was slight, but looked hungry. In the end, I knew I didn't care enough. I couldn't maintain the ball of anger that had grown in me. It didn't flare up inside, just kept me restless. On a low burn.
    Every now and then I see Adeline with Mattias, or with someone else, but if she tries to talk to me, I turn away. Do you get like that with those dogs that you know? If you could think at all, I wonder who you would be. Someone not cold? Someone away from the rain? A man without a dog?
    That's what I think sometimes, too.

One Summer Day of Change

Amy sat on the hard ground with her back against the wall. Her red floral dress had gradually rucked itself upwards until the hem sat just below her belly. Her exposed thighs were beginning to sweat against the pale green lino, in fact she was now beginning to feel a whole layer of grimy sweat stand out all over her, beneath her breasts and along her hairline. Danny sat crouched and wide-eyed in the corner opposite the washing machine, still not aware of what was really happening – something like this must just seem like a slight aberration for a seven year old, a small climax in the otherwise dreary lull of summer holidays.

Amy suddenly thinks she hears the ambulance approaching but then the sound is gone and she wonders whether or not it was actually ever there to begin with.

She thinks she gave the woman at the other end of the line the right address, the correct name. She thinks about ringing back to confirm the details but even now the three numbers she needs to dial have somehow slipped carefully from her mind like a dead green leaf falling to the ground. When she had called the woman on the other end of the line had asked her if she knew CPR and by that time Amy was crying and of course she had to say no. The conversation had come to a sudden end but Amy couldn't believe that that was the point of it all. She felt like nothing had been achieved because even when she tried to hang up the telephone (she had missed the receiver and the earpiece had scuttled off over the lino like a frightened insect) her eldest son Mathew remained motionless on the ground, his eyes sinking and his face turning steadily green outwards from the nose. The offending can of air freshener remained where it had fallen, just out of reach of his left hand, as if he may at any time suddenly jerk back to life and reach for it again.

She had not seen the boys for a while. She had been taking a break in the kitchen with a cup of Nescafé and the newspaper. She thought the kids were still out the back under the house mucking about with their bikes and tools. When she looked up Danny was standing against the kitchen doorway, one foot rubbing against the other, looking a bit confused and like he had done something wrong. She followed him out of the room good-humouredly wondering what on earth it could be this time.

It really was a very hot day, even the walls in the laundry (normally the coolest room in the house) were beginning to sweat. Slumped against the wall Amy saw now the thin metal door to the cupboard underneath the laundry sink was slightly open, she hadn't heard them open it she hadn't heard anything at all. The light blue flannel she kept in the cupboard for cleaning now protruded slightly out from underneath Mathew's neck. His small tough fingers remained motionless. A sheen of residue lay plastered over his nose and mouth from where he had sucked in the air freshener. The green and purple canopy of their big jacaranda tree peered in through the gap in the back door, but ultimately remained, regardless. Danny fidgeted a bit in the corner, unsure and maybe a bit scared of what to do next. He had been next in line to experiment with the aerosol can but as it was it did not turn out that way. Amy knew she should go to him and reassure him and tell him it wasn't his fault and that he hadn't done anything wrong but for the moment she couldn't do anything like that at all, she didn't think she could move from the spot where she had fallen. Danny had short-cropped blonde hair and was wearing a dark blue tank top just like his older brother who was now sprawled lifeless and still right across the middle of the laundry floor.

Amy put her hand to her temple and felt a shock of pain at the connection of skin. She moved her legs a little and felt the squelch of sweat between her thighs and the warm ground. Again she was sure she heard the ambulance but then it disappeared away again into the distant silent suburb. She watched the thick green on Mathew's face spread down along his neck and out across his shoulders and for the first ever time in her life felt truly terrified.

Letters to a Loved One

The last time I saw you, George, you were dead. Imprisoned in hospital light. Now I imagine things are dark for you, if they are anything at all.

We buried you near a eucalypt. On the day, sunlight was just how you adored it, with your eyes closed halfway, warmed in a wicker chair you had pushed out onto the dying grass. I never took much notice, except when oily clouds filtered the light and you frowned, adrift in the yard like a bird whose wings would not dry. I wish I had studied you, examined the shadow you cast or the restful gravity of your dangling limbs. As I look back, it is possible I believed I could have fallen asleep just by walking too near you or resting on the grass at your feet.

And you didn't see me, George – how could you, half asleep in your chair. I was part of an irritating world you observed only when it had darkened you with shade. If you saw me at all, it was looming over you, blackening your light.

I cannot remember how many years it has been since you died, although I know it has been many. The difference between living and dying does not seem significant any more. Who is dead and who is alive? I picture you pruning the roses that will outlive us all. I raked up the leaves from around your grave with my hands and put the longest stem in an old jar of water.

It seems a ridiculous fact to tell you, and perhaps you know already, but before I left the cemetery I lay down on your grave, the stone so cold beneath me, and stared up into the sky. Then I closed my eyes, trying to empty my mind of thoughts, but imagining how it could be that I would not exist, imagining an absence of everything. You know it better than I do, George, and I wish I could ask you. How foolish I would have seemed; an old woman lying on the grave of her dead husband.

Strangers now live in the house. Can you remember when we bought it, wondering about the lives housed by our wood and stone? So much of our lives is nothing. So many of us leave the world no different than how we found it. They haven't left much of the garden and I am told that they built a swimming pool over the grass you tended with such care and futility.

Thank Christ they left the rose beds.

That is how I still see you, pruning shears in your gloved hands, frowning with concentration, stems and thorns stacked at your feet.

Now our lives are the memories of door frames and window sills as others sweep the floors or polish the mantles. They can have it for it is only good for so long and after that it falls away to nothing. You know all this, George.

Many years ago there was a time when I had yet to meet you. It never occurred to you to ask what it might have been like, before you arrived so hopelessly dressed, but always with a carnation in your buttonhole. There were many hours when I did nothing but sit behind a closed door and stare at the ceiling, a pursuit that these days drives me to such acute boredom. What could there have been to think about? Whatever it was, there was no end of it, so much so that my adolescence seemed an age of unending contemplation.

'What can she be doing in there?' my mother asked to whoever would listen. 'Not even a sound.' I passed hours as if I was swimming laps.

There were men before you and, I imagine, women before me. They remained in the silent gulf between us. Whatever was left unspoken was left unchanged, as if we could not affect anything that we could not say. I could count half a dozen affairs that I almost had, those more beautiful than the one or two I did. At moments before falling asleep I thought of the bodies I collected in my heart, whose flesh I almost embraced, in that second when the adulterer commits the act in the heart, when her skin and muscles tighten with the unknown signs of that pleasure. Is that to say that I did not keep faith with you? I should say I did. How can years of ordinary bondage be tainted by a few hours of indecent pleasure? We had children, for Christ's sake; we came to more than hot air and perspiration, we came to more than the childish impatience of ravelled clothes. Before you it was simple, as if the touching of bodies had no meaning.

'What can she be doing in there?'

On summer evenings there was never more to do than to listen to the cicadas. How could I have explained that narcotic – all damp heat and the smell of flower-beds? Voices in the kitchen as women took turns at stirring the pots.

My father and the boys always returned after dark, swearing quietly in their exhaustion. You met him once, standing at the door; a strong, tall man of few words, who was happiest when he had something to lift or a hole to dig. That summer he was sinking a fence, digging trenches out near the edge of the bush, the sweat pouring off his blistered back. He laughed when I raised the mallet to drive in the guidepost, but I did it only to save the blisters weeping on his hands. He took the mallet from me and drove the post himself.

Silent action became a language between us, his huge hands picking me up, setting me down out of the way. The few words he did have set me on the path that wound up next to yours. If this letter were for him, I would thank him for that.

At the time I could have killed him for his terrific silence that could suffocate a room. He'd think we didn't notice, but we would be gasping for air. The boys understood it, even enjoyed it, out in the yard or the bush; they would follow him without need for speech. For me, silence came only with isolation, behind a closed door, half tucked up in a single sheet.

When men die, they do so loudly. They hallucinate, leap from their beds, argue, fight death with their fists. My father closed his eyes and died without a word, without even moving, as if death had been how he lived his entire life.

From those ashes you came, with an umbrella and a crumpled hat, standing in our doorway. Somehow it was my father's decision, the words of a man with no words. 'Get your coat and go with him. The poor boy's been waiting. Walked all this way when it wouldn't stop raining, so hurry before he falls to pieces on us.' Then my mother laughed. Do you remember? How she used to cover her teeth with her open hand whenever she laughed? Then Dad would grin his closed lipped grin. That is exactly how it was.

George, I don't know why I am writing to you. There nothing left for us to say. All the words are useless. It is as though I am talking to myself, which I can do without a pen or paper. Could I be putting everything in order, arranging the furniture in a room I will never see again? If so, how can I begin? The greatest art is sometimes silence. This means I should not begin.

But I am not beginning, for this is something that I could never have begun.

'Get your coat and go with him.'

Of everything I remember, there is one time I will make my last thought. I will remember an April of many years ago. There was a swamp with reeds and I was so young and small that I could lie on the reeds and they would support my weight above the water. The light came in through the trees. I fell asleep and woke when night had fallen. I will remember the weightlessness upon the reeds and the child I was, imagining it to be a throne. Carried above the heads of servants. Idle thoughts, George, but with a beautiful substance. Alone in the bush, suspended above the swamps, I listened to the singing of birds.

After the rain ended, I got my coat and went with you, smelling you all the way, a heavy scent somewhere near old, rotting wood. You drew me in close when we danced and somehow I was reassured by the weight of your cotton suit. Then it was months before I saw you again, because my father died. When I did, you didn't smile like you did the time before, but held my hand, as if you thought I might have fallen apart had you not been there to hold me together. At the time I thought you were like a word inserted into a sentence, one that had been, or should have been, forgotten. I often thought of you standing in the doorway, soaked through. Then you became all the sentences I understood.

Outside the window I can see into the garden, or imagine I can. I am sitting at the old kitchen table, the ancient cloth spread across it. There can be no explanation for it, but I made up my face and did my hair before sitting down. Later I will visit your grave and deliver your mail.

The best time is in the evening when the shadows of the trees have grown long and the funeral crowds have gone. Head stones turn red in the sun, especially the ornate statues that tower above us. When the light is like that I look around, wrap my coat tightly and lie myself down on your grave. Just the sound of leaves and the wind in uncut grass.

Then I long for that moment to be upon me, the thought of harsh swamp reeds cutting my skin, the darkness falling on me and the first feel of – I will try the word – of dying.

George, where are you when these thoughts eat me alive? Why do I hunger for the stone of your plot behind my back and just enough sun so that it still warms me?

Damn it, George, you know more about it than I ever could, but I know it so well. I will go there. The time will come, whether I am ready or afraid. The time will come when shadows cast themselves. They will fall without light, darkness, ground, or walls. They will fall upon themselves in a world they comprise alone. Nothing can stop it and that, finally, becomes the tragedy.

I am now everything that I ever was. It is enough, George, for the words fail me. In the entire world there are so many saying so much, so much and so little. Now the words are useless, so I must end. Goodbye, I say, though to whom, I do not know. Goodbye.

Pettifer

1.

Pettifer often dreamed about naked women. At night in the dark he would sit crunched and hollowed and look through his front window wondering what he would do if ever a woman should walk past and then whether he could ever summon up the courage to burst from his house and say hello.

At these times he drank weak beige tea infused with thin drops of bitter lemon.

He owned no pets. He buried his cat Misty last year out the back in the hard ground underneath the silent jacaranda tree.

2.

Pettifer's shoulders were already hunched a little underneath the thin sharp wire of his moustache. His brittle fingers curled towards the corners of his elbows from the sudden end of his pressed black suit. His hair was black and straight and wet, always wet, like he had forever been sweating underneath the damp velvet of his bowler hat. There was a space between his two front teeth. His lips were two pale lines drawn across a sharp face.

He had been involved in an unpleasant experience at a Chinese restaurant. Through sheer accident he had twice been given the wrong dish. The second time he had thrown the boiling soup over the waiter's face. His own face had turned red in patches and he had unfortunately spat in a silver line down the edge of his pointed chin.

His suit had separated over his white shirt. His neck was thin and marked with knuckles. As he stood there seething watching the screaming waiter writhe with pain he thought about one day paying for a blowjob.

3.

He occasionally found himself crying into the small pile of bricks he had stored for some reason at the back of his house. He remembered it always resulted with the simultaneous taste of salt and sand in the hole of his mouth. He sometimes wished for the imagination to feel hopeless.

4.

She was nothing special but Pettifer had followed her home one night. Home turned out to be an old abandoned art gallery. He watched for a while then broke in. He discovered there was the outside wall and then all around an inside wall a few feet in.

To hang up the art, Pettifer thought, and sniggered. He bit down hard on the base of his middle finger to quiet himself.

5.

She had had rats before but this was different. If she sat still there was nothing, but a few moments after she moved there was always a resulting scuffle behind the walls. Eventually, with a small black and red hand drill, she punched a hole in the wall, near one corner of the main room.

She stood a few steps back from the new hole in the wall, hands on hips, the skewed drill bit pointing downwards toward the ground. After a short time a small wide bloodshot eye shuffled hesitantly into view.

6.

Soon after she went outside and sealed up all possible exits with concrete and bricks. Pettifer had forgotten how he had broken in but it was a wise precaution.

She drilled more holes but only ones big enough for eyes, she had no desire to encompass an entire face. She imagined holes in the bathroom would be favourites so she only placed a couple of those in strategic positions. She occasionally pushed through food; olives and breadsticks.

She shook her short blonde hair around and spun in a slow circle.

7.

She always touched herself delicately at first before increasing the tempo and losing control. She was careful not to make love at home but dinner parties were never interrupted. The new design in her house (the holes in the walls) was considered unique and individual.

She looked at herself in the mirror and raised her arms above her head. Her breasts were shaped with letters and her clean white side cut through the air.

8.

Pettifer's fingernails grew into horns, his tongue turned to plaster. He thought one day he'd finally lick through to her, if only he just kept trying.

Epistle on his Ninety Third Year

I had the impression that I was emerging from the background, a relief figure, that his eyes recognised me slowly because they were not equipped to sense the way I suddenly darkened the white walls of the room. The thoughtless focus of his eyes drifted over the brown assembly of furniture, and then settled on me finally, as though I had just appeared square in front of him, a shade that had abruptly accumulated human mass.

At first, he did not speak, nor did he raise his hand in recognition, as I would have expected. I allowed myself to follow his slow, unmeasured breathing, the mechanics of rising and falling as I watched it half concealed in his chest. I sat in the high backed chair and waited.

I imagined I was visiting myself as an old man. I closed my eyes and saw the fragile weight of my bones, the spindles of my arms, the way an antiseptic nurse rearranged the pillows. Then there was the harshness of light as I woke and opened my eyes. Then finding before me a young man with wide eyes, holding his hat in his hands and shifting his weight from one foot to the other.

Eventually, he spoke.

'Where's the leather coat I had?' he asked. Perhaps the cold reminded him. I knew at once he was speaking to himself. It was possible he imagined himself to be a young man visiting a dying patient; he sometimes looked at me as if to say, what would I think, what would I become, if I could be you once more? 'Beautiful ox blood leather that reached your knees. As far as that.' He moved his hand, imagining it touched his leg. 'Then it just fell apart – fell apart at the seams and no-one would fix it for fear of ruining the leather. I never understood it. Never understood why they never put it back together. I wore it down every street north of the river, passing all the women you could pass so that your hat never touched your head. Those days were never long enough.' His eyes closed as he summoned up an autumn day from within himself; the trees that shed their leaves and sunlight that couldn't penetrate the leather of his coat. What could I say to help him? I could never have pretended to know him, to know how fragile a man becomes as he looks back over his hundred years, as though everything he could recall was weighed against him. A leather coat? Nothing to a young man, but he understood that; his own leather coat was nothing to him once.

His eyes drifted closed as he fell asleep again.

Instead of waiting, I took to my feet and fled into the hallway. A nurse had moved into his house and sat half asleep in a chair beside the door. A thin stream of dancehall music played on a small radio. The nurse looked up at me and smiled, as if she could have reassured me. I couldn't breath. My heart hammered in my throat. I leant forward and could see him drawn up tightly in his bed, his lips taut across his open mouth. I leant back against the wall, afraid of the room, unsettled by the rattle of the hospital trolley someone was preparing in the kitchen and the vague light squaring in from the street lamps. I cursed the old man for the thoughts he had driven into my head – why should I be thinking of death? Why had he no other fool to sit by his side and wait?

Mr Vincent was once a tall, straight man where now he was bent out and dying. His body had once angled up into his grey hair and green eyes, strong thin arms and muscular legs carried his weight without effort. I studied the fingers that I had so often seen rest on the strings of a violin. His genius had been caged within the moving ribs that were coming to a standstill.

His body was as weightless as the memories it contained – the sallow stain of it pressed into the starched sheets. I entered the room again and fell back into the chair.

He drew a cup to his lips and wet his mouth. His trembling hands traced figures in the air as he spoke, then fell abruptly by his sides. At times he murmured, and I leant in close to hear the set of unrelated phrases – the nonsense – passing his lips. Can the expressions streaming from the dry mouth of a dying man have meaning? As he spoke, it was as if he was caught in the net of an hallucination. I don't know when he began or when he stopped, only that we had fallen out of focus, as though we ourselves melted into his meaningless words, as though he had manufactured a world into which we both fell.

A heat came in suddenly with the air and I realised that I had been waiting in a room that gripped me as heavy and as dark as a fur coat. Molly sat outside on the veranda and I couldn't say why she didn't come in except that she was drunk. I'd seen her drinking bottles of beer as she sat in an old tyre that hung from the plane tree, her pale dress up over her knees. But I waited for her, remembering the way she'd brought the bottle to her lips and looked up at you through her eyebrows. If I'd been sober, I would have gone out to look for her, to let my head fall into her lap and close my eyes. I would have waited, my arms around her waist, my mouth full of her cotton dress.

I remember thinking, this is why I'm here, this is why I'm alive – to have her so close, to die next to the rising and falling of her chest, to feel her greasy fingers trace patterns on my naked back.

She tossed the empty bottles into a rusted out drum that we used to burn the newspaper stacks my uncle left me. After her fifth beer, she stumbled up to the back door and called for me, leaning her head against the flyscreen. Then she slid down to the wooden boards of the veranda, swearing at me because she thought I'd locked the door. Soon after, I could hear the deep breaths that she forced out when she was asleep. Now and then, she would stir, roll into a new position, just as uncomfortable as the last, and then fall back into her thorough, restless sleep.

I look back on all these recollections, nothing in themselves. I sift through them, but cannot understand them; I am ignorant beneath the burden of their abstract significance. Sifted through the mesh of age, what is the use? Why remember these people, or these insignificant events? You are too young and too fit to know. When you come here, you can't understand. Those with strong legs have no need for memories; they move from one room into the next, then outside into the ton of sunlight. All the fragments I recall cannot burden you, overbear you, because your limbs are strong. I am the contrail of a man, with the blankets drawn up to my neck, unable to move.

I remember the next day. We took a long walk, out with our pounding heads and thick useless tongues. Molly and I, we were never wholly beneath the shade of the eucalypt trees. I counted each step until we were staring down the scarp into the trickling brown shaft of the river.

'You know you're alive after that,' she said, pointing back down the embankment and the half trodden track. I waited until I caught my breath and worked my hands around her waist, as though she might have lost her footing. She brought her open mouth up against mine, where I tasted the wet ash and alcohol of the night before. Then she leaned away from me. Laughter filled her eyes and, at last, I understood that she was more complex than she had led me to believe; I fooled myself that she was laughing at me and that there was an intelligence in her mockery, a cunning brilliance in the way she turned the light from her eyes.

Without warning, an inexplicable anger broke over me like hot water. I gripped her hair and forced back her head. Her startled eyes peered up into the sky as the oily rage permeated my flesh.

'I don't need you to tell me I'm alive,' I said to her without raising my voice. She murmured something I could not hear through her parted lips and I released her. 'Don't be fucking stupid.'

We walked back in silence and sat on the veranda, cradling cold bottles of beer, but neither of us drinking. I swore to myself that I would not ask her for forgiveness, even after the fury had peeled off my skin like old paint, an indecent flaking of everything that in that instant I had suddenly become. For a moment, I wished I'd gripped her throat. It was as though nothing fitted together; every action, every movement of the lips, was a piece of wreckage strewn from an accident. I could not reconcile the furious life that had sprung up in my hands with the churning violence of my heart. In all of my life, I had never known such unease. Molly stared at me with her slow blinking eyes, full of the deliberate intelligence I had just discovered and the anger she failed to disguise as pity. I stole glances at her, willing her to stop, longing for her to stare at the ground so I could disintegrate into the crumpled wreck I was becoming. The day ended and grew dark. Then she reached her hand out to me and we embraced, as though the night had eclipsed everything that had happened between us.

With all the strength I had, I forced my hands to be patient. I undressed her slowly, so that the sum of the whole was revealed in parts, none of which relied any of the others. In the darkness, there was no account of time; we were lost and adrift, dulled by the heat, slippery in each other's lethargic hands. I imagined myself in the elemental power of the sea as she rolled herself beneath me like the mechanics of the swell. I was not myself, not a man with flesh and blood, but a ghost suddenly alive in the grey rising of her limbs. She had left the radio on and the tin foil echo of violin music somehow reached me through the murk; the timbre of the instrument was like a hand reaching for me through the dark.

And now the music returns to me, more so than the woman. It is a force hidden in the atmosphere, so I think of it whenever my mind comes to rest. I can picture the musician, his eyes closed, the violin distending from him like another limb upon which his hand delicately moves. I hear each note through the speaker of the transistor, each one an inseparable part of the one before. In my mind, I match the rising and falling of the music to what I can recall of her body; its movement, strength and the copious perfume that sprang from her like an animal.

I was not awake, not fully aware of her, until it was over. I could not remember entering the room that came into focus. She appeared before me; naked, unravelled, as though every part of her had loosened as she tumbled into sleep, her mouth coming open with a smile as she drifted away, lights still over her from the dusty globes we couldn't be bothered switching off. I did not sleep. I was too astonished by the physical memory of her body wrapping itself around my utter being, as though I had been a ball she had carried in her fist.

The music consumes my memory of that day, but I see also her profound nakedness, the way her body took on meaning. When everything else I could of remembered had been forgotten, then she appeared, falling asleep beside me, our bodies still awash with each other.

When she woke, she leapt from the bed and quickly dressed, as though she was furious. She refused to look at me until she stood on the threshold of the corridor, then she turned towards the bed and stared for a moment at the room, not taking in any part of it, but consuming it all with wide eyes.

'You should be ashamed of yourself,' she said, remembering her hair and trying to fix it in place with one hand. 'You're a bastard, Vincent. A smooth, calculating bastard.'

How should I have reacted? I did not understand it, but I did not care; I would have laughed as soon as fall to my knees, but then she was gone, so I stared at the paint peeling from the ceiling, thinking of myself and how old I had suddenly become, even though it was just a few brutal hours.

At the end of it all, the imperfect reach of the memory falls short of life's corpulence. What secrets expired with his flesh? Could an old radio and the violence of his desire put everything in its place, put him to rest as though he had drawn up his confession in certain terms? There was nothing more he could have uttered, no last words beyond the tight knot of recollection. A private death, I thought, behind the hospital curtain they had set up around his bed. Perhaps he had unburdened himself merely through the exhausting act of breathing, rearranging his mouth with every expiration to calm the turmoil of his mind.

I never knew because the vigour in his eyes went out like a light. He sunk into the silence that seized his flesh completely. He had fallen into the death we suffer before the body dies, became an open mouthed corpse that sucked in small breaths through lips kept moist by the towel I ran over them.

I thought of him as he might have been in a leather coat, leaning against a street lamp, hat cocked over one eye, and waiting for a woman. I had been prepared for a revelation. He had prepared me for that, but it never came. I had come to know the few hours that had been stirred up within him, as though they were more than just an hallucination.

Music still played on the radio – I could barely hear it – even though a different nurse sat in the chair near the door. Suddenly, I was overwhelmed with a sickness. My stomach churned at the thought of all the men who were dying in the world, and not just those who filled the hospital rooms, but those who walked the streets and sat behind desks, those who had just fallen asleep. I thought of my last hour, the thoughts that could burden my mind. I stood and bid Mr Vincent goodbye. This dying man had once been so alive and I could not comprehend any of it.

I came back the next day to see that he was worse off yet again. I lay my hands over his face and wonder now whether somehow he had been conscious – had he felt my trembling fingers, the coldness that had overwhelmed me? I kissed his forehead and said nothing as I left. I never returned to the room, but waited to read the obituary that I supposed had already been written.

When they buried him, I watched from my car as the hearse drove through the gates, then was lost, a sea of dark coats pacing slowly behind it. I turned away, imaging the possibility of his corpse, hammered shut inside the coffin.

The Tuesday following I went to the grave and touched the dirt with my fingers because I remembered he had made his ninety third year. The flowers still had not wilted, perhaps because the rain had not stopped.

The Chetlands

1.

Ason walks slowly away to the far paddock with Belle lolling quietly by his side. Ason's great black walking stick, which reaches from its gnarled foot to just above his head, thumps heavily along on his left side like a trunk or a single limb of its own accord. Belle glances through the washes of fog occasionally but for the most part seems uninterested.

Ason is sad yet relieved in ways, walking heavily with his wide head bent towards the ground. The situation, he knows, is sinful, has been drenched with sin ever since the gentle beginnings. Ason suspects the time has come for him to act upon his disgrace and to end the relationship and all its associated immoralities. If Ason hopes for a salvation of sorts he knows it will only be in this lifetime. It is as he expects – the more he tried to deny it the more weight he gave to the idea that sin is never completely hidden, no matter how deep the affection behind closed doors. As a moral man, or perhaps more as a man who wants again to believe in himself as moral, he knows he is making the right decision.

But consequently he is also aware that now there will only be an empty damp bed and the stone cold walls at night to keep him company. As he continues to walk he is surrounded by the thought of the endless evenings ahead, watching time slide slowly by like the impenetrable loneliness of an autumn afternoon.

He moves disconsolately through the pathways of his farm with Belle walking by his side, two dark figures shuffling across the land.

2.

They reach the gate eventually, Ason and Belle, the front gate to the back paddock. The gate is an hesitant unstable thing with bent pieces of wire limply holding old planks of rotten wood together. In silent communication they both stop still at the same time – and wait for a moment, unaffected. Ason lifts his tired head and gazes across the land. The back fence of the

37

farm is not visible from the front gate for the back paddock stretches away and out of sight down a long gentle incline. The landscape is lumped with hills and gullies and all is covered with a thick green grass from here. The atmosphere is sodden and damp. The rounded hills seem pressed down into themselves and squat thick bushes remain unmoved by the ever-present chill of the wind. The breeze blows cold and shrill and the dark green tops of a few struggling trees huddle close together.

Ason keeps a pack of Chetland dogs, known simply as Chetlands. They are grey to black haired dogs without tails. They are big creatures, about the size of fully grown hyenas, but unlike those animals Chetlands are apathetic, slow beasts, their general demeanour creating a regardless atmosphere of ambivalence. They have black faces, deep slow black eyes and their diet consists solely of grass. Today, as always, they stand silent, dotted around the paddock like statues. A few plod laconically through the damp foliage, or swing their heads rakingly from side to side, surveying the ground.

Ason carefully lifts up the wire latch on the front gate and moves Belle through into the descending back paddock. She pads away, past groups of three or four dogs standing quiet and still in the cold breeze under the grey sky. She moves away, the edges of her thick coat already dampening on the wet dense grass. She doesn't look back, but swings her black face once or twice to either side.

Ason is glad, or maybe not – as he stands solid in the thickening fog he is already hearing the broken room and the empty bed waiting sadly at home for his return.

3.

A few days ago Ason found himself at the local tavern where thick cigarette smoke replaced the fog of the fields and grey old men from the community sat and talked while the yellow froth of beer hung from their beards. The drenched white coasters on the bar were so wet with use they had turned almost to sponge.

From somewhere within the dull musty atmosphere of the pub someone asked Ason why he kept Chetlands (the common opinion being they were a useless breed to keep in such a heavily productive rural area). The old gnarled hands wrapped around the beers waited and listened.

'I don't know', Ason shrugged, aware and upset that his secret may have been uncovered at last. He fumbled in the loose store of his brain for a response. 'Keeps the grass down I guess'.

In reply the stuffy yellow atmosphere shifted slightly and within its silence Ason felt the disgusted sting of accusation. Although in fact the town folk were not at all aware of Ason's intimate relationship with Belle, based on his own fears of impropriety he imagined they were, and he interpreted within their eyes and shoulders a sudden verdict of social and human disgrace.

It can be no other way, Ason thought then, I have ruined myself with my own weak lust. He left the tavern hunched and broken, a shamed and guilty man perforated with confusion.

He walks home now from the far paddock, thinking of Belle and not much else. He is a large man, getting wider and thicker the further he goes down. The black tangled hair of his head and beard matches the sleeveless wool apron he wears that stretches from his shoulders to his heavy leather shoes. His hips are wider than his shoulders and his legs are immense. His tall stick which he uses to balance his walk also gets larger the further it goes down, a trunk or limb of its own accord which at inconsistent intervals thumps along the ground with its great round foot of wood. Ason walks, trudging heavily along the path and smelling on the horizon the familiar smell of incoming rain. He walks with his black eyes lowered and his breathing quiet. He is a large man and the damp soil path he walks along remains unmoved by his long leaden sigh….

4.

There is a particularly heavy windstorm that night, one that threatens the stone and abuses the planks of Ason's small square house. In the middle of the night Ason walks outside and stands face on into the thrashing gale. Behind him the small poor house flails about with its windows and shutters that have been battered loose from their lodgings by the furious wind. Ason would not stand a chance out in the open field, he would be rocked and flattened like a pebble.

He thinks of nothing but Belle as the relentless careless wind sends his coarse hair lashing across his face. Her strong thick coat would protect her along with the presence of the other dogs who always clump tight together on nights like this, circling and shuffling so the group keeps moving, never leaving one animal on the outside for too long. (He has an image of Belle as the centre point from which all the other animals emanate and circle while she remains still and safe in the middle of a strongly protected cocoon). He thinks of all the other dogs bodies pressed up against hers as they remember her smell, her shape, the curve of her stomach that angles gently up towards the strong posts of her back legs. He thinks of a giant hateful gust of wind scooping the whole pack of them up in a stubborn hand and carelessly flinging them all as one to the very driest unreachable ends of the earth. He thinks of never holding her again, of never again feeling the tender collapse of her body upon his smooth entry into her and the soft resulting growl that always escaped her. He wonders of this accursed black night and if it will ever end.

Ason stands singular, cut off from everything outside his own vision. The impersonal wind, with no regard for feelings other than its own empty hands, continues to abuse and taunt his aching body and compound his thickening fears.

5.

(He cannot do it, he has neither the will nor the desire to be alone and judgement be damned). Early the next cold morning Ason walks determinedly through the broken aftermath of the windstorm. Thick trees have cracked, whole paddocks seem to have shifted off their centre and, although long dead, shattered wings of broken birds flap lightly in the remnants of the breeze.

Delirious from the lack of sleep, Ason watches his thick black haired hands unlatch the gate to the far paddock. He scans the grass paths for Belle, but all the dogs seem to have congregated at the back end of the field. Ason moves hurriedly over the thick grass in the direction of the pack and given the lazy uninterested nature of the breed he is soon at the tail end of them.

He sees where they are heading. The sky is still and grey again. The windstorm has destroyed a portion of the back fence and the dogs are moving steadily in a slow procession through the break. He pushes his way through the slow heaving numbers, scanning their coats and backs unsuccessfully for any sign of Belle. As there is no increased fever in the dogs attempt to escape he soon reaches the fallen portion of the fence. He halts the procession abruptly by standing in the middle of the break with his legs wide apart and his great stick held with both hands high above his head. His breathing is heavy and full but otherwise he remains silent. The dog's left in the paddock stop where they are and look uncaringly at him out of their deep black eyes set in their deep black faces.

He can see no sign of Belle.

He manages to round a few of the last unperturbed escapees back into the paddock then stabilises the fallen fence enough to create a satisfactory barrier. The remaining dogs quickly lose interest and return casually to their slow silent grazing of the field.

Ason is outside the paddock now, on the far side of the back fence. A few disappearing Chetland hulks can be seen moving far down the thickly grassed hill and beyond that into the untouched tangled forest of these parts. Ason feels a wide space opening inside him, bigger than the farm, larger in fact than anything he has ever known. On a distant ridge a line of grey fat rain drops on to the forest and shields off the rest of the land and the sky behind.

6.

His feet have taken root. The grass slowly curls around the foot of his stick. The dogs behind him stand still in the rain with their thick heads lowered and their coarse coats beginning to sag underneath the force of the down-pour. The grey rain and the lash of the returning wind have made his eyes water and his skin hurt but he stands his ground, scanning through the waves the dense horizon. Far away in the sky a few black birds punctuate the blank page.

Mr Black, Goodbye

She had been stirred up in Mister Black again, like the dry mouth of an addiction. Her image would not shift from the back of his throat. It was a dust cloud that moved through his living carcass, enraging those parts of him that had been dead for years. He stepped from the bus and tried to catch his breath, frightening himself with the quickened thumping of his heart.

Mister Black was a fat man with closely cropped grey hair. When he spoke his voice quivered as if it was breaking and his brow furrowed into many deeply etched creases.

Through the glass of the grocery shop window, he could see her wipe the counter clean with a cloth. Her hair was tied back and he felt a sharpness in that disappointment. Usually it hung limp in its darkness about her shoulders and he would glimpse at her until the sunlight caught the shine of it. He didn't care for the rest of her, though he told himself that he was keeping a distance that was appropriate for a man his age. He could not control, however, the thoughts that drained the blood from his skull, the loose sphinctered desire that emerged from deep within his gut when he imagined her hair falling over his white, corpulent thighs.

It's all about keeping the appropriate distance, he told himself, even as he longed to bring himself closer.

He made sure the bell on the door rang loudly as he sponged his weight through it. His belly was a dead weight, stretching the capacity of his cotton shirt.

He knew her name was Sarah. She was tall with green eyes and was embarrassed by her long, awkward limbs and her red fingers that she hid deep in her pockets when she wasn't stacking shelves or counting the till.

'Good morning,' he called to her and she nodded, raising her palm to him in recognition. He moved around the shop, filling his basket with fruit, listening to the echo his feet made in the empty aisles.

Distance is an abstraction, he reasoned with himself. She is a grown woman, capable of thinking for herself, thinking the thoughts of a grown woman. She is an adult who knows a comfortable distance. He emptied his basket onto the counter in front of her, resting his hands there also. Light came at her through the window. She weighed the fruit quickly, keen to return her hands to the warm darkness of her coat.

'Hello there, Sarah.' He tried her name in his mouth, hoping it would come out deeply, but instead it tapered off in a child's falsetto.

''Morning. You're Mister Black aren't you?' She glanced up and noticed his head leaning over to one side so he could see her hair that was drawn back and tied behind her neck. 'I was in the same year as your daughter.'

'Oh, that would have been a few years ago now.' He fought the urge to touch her hand. A network of veins was visible beneath the surface of her skin. Other times he had not spoken to her so she would cast her eyes down and turn to the cash register. Her hair would fall on her shoulders and down her back. When she turned away he could not recall the colour of her eyes.

'Yeah, it's been a while. How is she? I've not seen her for ages.'

'I wouldn't see her much more than you, I suppose. Her mother tells me she's fine. Off at university she tells me.'

'I thought she'd do well.'

Mister Black huffed while she packed his groceries into a paper bag. She glanced at him again and saw he was studying her arms. Suddenly her skin shivered, as though someone was breathing on her neck. His age, his moist lips, the webbing of veins around his nose, all disgusted her. She imagined herself pushing him away, but feeling his dry hands on her prickling flesh, holding up her forearms to prevent the descent of his jowls onto her breasts. Part of her pitied him, thought him sad.

'I hope you wouldn't be offended if I told you something personal,' he said, looking down at his own hands. 'I like your hair better when you wear it down.' His face was usually an ill white, but he felt the sudden heat of blood beneath his eyes as he blushed.

Sarah laughed, covering her mouth with her hand. Even the old women who came in every day had told her the same thing, reaching up their hands to touch the dark mane that stretched down her back.

'You have beautiful hair,' Mister Black said. 'Make sure you look after it.'

'I wash it every day.'

Mister Black drew a breath deep into his lungs and pictured himself through her eyes; an old man with watery eyes, her friend's father shuffling through the house she had visited once or twice.

'This may seem like a strange thing to ask,' he began, 'but there is a reason for it, so please hear me out. Would you let me photograph your hair? I am practically a professional. I wouldn't charge you a cent, though. Because you're a friend of the family.' She has the right to refuse, thought Mister Black. She is a young woman who knows her own limits.

Sarah fought for the words to refuse, opened her mouth, but she said nothing and drew a breath. She sensed a lightness in her belly, a shock that anyone could ask a question that was so complex, with so many variables.

'Don't say no yet,' he said, just as she began to mumble. 'There's a reason, a good one, too. You might not believe it, but I was young once. I met a girl on the coast when I went for a holiday years ago. You are the spitting image; you look just like her, especially your hair. You both wear it down the same way, how it tumbles everywhere. She moved to England before I told her how I felt and never had the courage to write to her. I just wish I had a photo to remember her by. You would fix an old man's broken heart.' He closed his mouth and waited for her to speak. They could both hear the labour of his breathing.

At that moment the bells on the door rang and the two old women came into the shop, shuffling towards the counter against which Mister Black leaned.

'Well?' he pressed Sarah. Her face had begun to flush. 'There's no harm in it, just a favour for an old man, eh?' She said nothing, but impatiently nodded her head. What if women rushing towards them heard of it? She took a pencil from the till and wrote her address and a time one week from that day. Then the old ladies were upon them in a cloud of musty perfume. Mister Black took his grocery bags and left the shop, the scrap of paper pressing into his sweating palm. She could have said no, he reassured himself. Its all a question of keeping the proper distance.

The bells rang again as he passed out of the shop. Through the window he glimpsed her hair and the frown that darkened her face as she stared at her feet and nodded to the old women, secretly waiting for him to disappear.

Sarah woke early and washed her hair, feeling the weight of it full of water as she wrung it out over the sink. She tidied her flat, washed the dishes and left a radio on, it's volume so low she could barely hear it. The image of his thick lips recurred in her mind, the thin voice emerging as they parted and she could see his brown and broken teeth. Her eyes could not settle on the book she had picked up, so she instead studied her hands, turning them over and over in the light that split the half closed curtains.

Hours passed slowly while she waited for him. It would be possible to hide in the room and not open the door, she thought, to bury her head in her hands, but he would soon be back in the shop, his fleshy wounded face accusing her. All he could take was a moment and then he would be gone.

She posed before the mirror and examined herself, letting her hair fall around her face. She widened her eyes and inspected her teeth, leaning close into the glass.

When his knuckles rapped the front door, she leapt to her feet and opened the door. Mister Black stood there with a camera case and a coat hung over his shoulder.

'Hello, again,' he said. She mumbled and stepped aside as she let him through the door.

He put his camera case on a table that filled the room, undid its leather straps and began to assemble his camera. He thanked her without looking at her and she leant against the doorframe watching him.

He looked across at her. 'You look perfect. Exactly how I remember her. People don't do it these days, but she used to dye her hair with beetroot and your colour is almost exactly the same.' Sarah's hair had a red tint to it.

His eyes focussed on a point beyond the walls.

'I don't dye my hair at all,' said Sarah, looking down at her feet as she worked the carpet with her toes.

Mister Black's skin was pale and dry. The colour had run from his jowls and his long lashes and watery eyes made him look as if he was falling asleep. By the time he had screwed the lens into the camera, Sarah had pulled a chair out from the table and was sitting opposite him. He directed the lens against the wall, adjusting the focus and pretending for the moment that he was alone in his room, that he was not consumed by her presence.

He had collected the money to arrive by taxi by emptying the tins in which he saved his coins. He had been buckled by the thought of her all the way to her flat. The thought of being close to her made him shut his eyes and tighten the muscles of his back. Bringing his hand up to cover his face, he had groaned, his mind extinguished of all thoughts except for her hair and how he imagined it would fall out across her naked back.

As he focussed the camera, Sarah studied him, embarrassed by his old stained shirt that couldn't be tucked in at the back. She could see his flaccid, hairless gut through the buttons. His tumid lips disgusted her.

'Let's start,' he said, getting to his feet. He looked around the room at the light, considering where best it would catch her. Finally, he asked her to stand near the wall that faced a bright open window.

She makes me feel alive, he thought as he lined her up in the camera, feeling the lightness of his heart. The blood is pumping again, my heart cannot stop the way it hammers in my chest. He told himself he had never been so far from death with this woman standing before him, exercising the freedom of her will. She could have said no, he thought. But she didn't. He felt perverse in the pleasure he wore like a suit, allowing it to straighten his back and frowning as she waited.

'Like this?' she asked, holding her arms out from her body and expecting him to direct her into a pose.

'Just stand naturally. Like you normally would.'

She tried to relax her body, but her muscles stiffened and her arms would not fall comfortably. She felt as though she was naked and had the urge to lay her wrists across her breasts. Then she was consumed by the camera's flash, which surprised her, so she closed her eyes. Mister Black took a step backwards and caught her again, making sure her eyes were still closed. She listened to the mechanical workings of the camera, waiting for him to stop so she could find herself in another position. He crossed the room and photographed her in profile.

As her eyes opened, he photographed her again, hoping he had caught something of the surprise in her face, hoping he had captured the moment just as her eyes were opening.

'Through here,' he said and walked into the next room. She followed him. 'What I want you to do is flick your hair up, so I'll get it in mid air.' She tossed it with her fingers while her photographed her. 'Don't use your hands, just throw your head.'

As Sarah closed her eyes again, she sensed a shallowness within herself, as if she had become nothing other than the images he captured. Thoughtlessly and without feeling his hands, she allowed him to rearrange her limbs, adjust her clothes and disarrange her hair to set her in the poses he required. She had become a manakin he manipulated with quick movements of his hands. He had her bend forward, her hair falling over her face, her hands resting on her knees.

A confidence and complexity rose within Mister Black. The woman posed on the instructions that he alone had the power to issue as he was the one operating the deceit of the camera. The weaknesses he imagined in himself fell away as he lined her up in the crosshairs; his voice became assertive and he spoke with fewer words.

'I'm almost there,' he said, pausing to change the film. 'A few more and I'm done.'

He took the final shots after he had taken several of her blank face, her dark hair falling over her ears and, he suspected, a grey shadow of hatred falling across her eyes. She had given her consent, he reminded himself. I wouldn't be here if she didn't. As he took apart the camera and began to pack it away in its case, he became aware that she was glaring at him. He glanced at her and saw her furrowed brow set resolutely above her eyes. Her mouth was also wrinkled.

'Will you send me copies?' she asked. He agreed, nodding his head nervously, his confidence dismantled by the hardness she had acquired. He waved his hand and inclined his head towards her, still bent over the table.

'Of course,' he said. 'Its part of the bargain.' He felt conspicuous, even with his back turned to her. It was as though she had undressed him and was examining him coldly, without compassion, her attention burning across those places that were beginning to be starved of oxygen. He had the urge to run from the room, to not look back as she stared after him.

He thanked her and walked through the flat to the front door, not waiting for her to show him out, or to see if she had even followed him through the room. He turned and nodded to her as he stepped over the threshold and closed the door behind himself.

'Goodbye,' he said again quietly to himself after he hurried down the stairs and spilled out onto the footpath.

In the hours after he had disappeared, Sarah studied the flaws in herself as though her eyes and her mind were detached from the sordidness of her body. Every faint scar, every blue vein, the subtle asymmetry of her face were all lit up before the sharpness of her self-criticism. As she again examined herself in the mirror, she imagined the blood draining from her body, as though her throat had been cut. She imagined her heart had stopped beating and closed her eyes to see darkness rather than the obvious unevenness of her eyebrows.

She shuddered, imagining he was still close to her. Had she the courage, she would not have answered the door, but she had been compelled to open it, interested and angry with herself. Mister Black had taken rights over her, moved through her flat as if it was his own. She saw his clumsy fat fingers struggling with the camera, the closely cropped white stubble of his head. She reminded herself that he had gone before she dressed herself for work, resigned to the inevitable boredom of the afternoon shift, dreading that she had so much time to think about him; she tried to shut him out of her mind.

Days later, the package arrived. She left it on the table until she had showered and changed then, holding it out with her fingers, felt it for weight, studied the stamps, the frayed corners and the small, neat hand writing he had left on the face of it. Then, suddenly, she tore open the end and slid out the packet of photographs. She thumbed through them. Even though they had colour, she was humourless and without life. She thought she even looked surprised, as though the situation in which she had found herself was astonishing, more than frightening, more than bizarre.

She turned them upside down on the table and covered them with her hands. The network of veins ran from her knuckles past her wrists and up her arms. She held her breath to reassure herself that her heart was still beating and that the blood was still rushing in her ears. Unsure, she closed her eyes.

Everything played over and over again in his mind like a sallowness spreading through his brain. He pictured her limp and lifeless, but at least, he reassured himself, she had not laughed. She had let him in of her own free will. She had stood there, not smiling, an empty slate, waiting for him to walk away from her and through the door.

Memories returned to him as he sat on the bus, feeling its movement through his legs. He had caught the bus years before, taken it to the coast, seeing himself alive on it, breathing in the air as if it was a drug. The feeling of salt was never washed from his skin. He despised the dryness of his hands, the tightness that stretched in his throat as he wandered along the beaches, the laughter of so many people that seemed to fill the air and rise like a fog from the pubs.

Two women had caught his attention and he followed them to the beach. They smiled at him as he threw his towel down near them and they called over to him, waving their hands as if to beckon him to join them. He sat between them as if he was a king, imagining secretly that he ruled the empire of their flesh. They laughed when he tried to make them laugh, but caught him off guard when they reached a secret accord between themselves, sprang to their feet, pulled off their bathing suits and ran naked into the water. They turned to him and called, again beckoning him to follow them, but his joints fused and he furrowed his brow.

Emptiness stirred within him. He could not follow them. Looking back years later, he was at a loss to explain why he could not strip of his shorts and run after them, into the cold surf up to his neck. Instead, he watched them swim out over the reef and wait until he disappeared from their sight before running up the beach and covering themselves with their towels. The way that Sarah, the assistant in the grocery shop, reminded him of the older girl made him almost ill.

He stepped off the bus a stop earlier than usually he would, his head still slick with memory. He walked a few hundred yards into town.

Out of breath, he stood across the road from the grocery shop and stared through the window, not caring who saw him. Sarah leant at the counter and stuffed a young man's groceries into a bag, parting her lips wide as she spoke to him. Never mind, thought Mister Black, she came of her own free will. No one forced her. It could have been much worse for both of us.

Even after twenty minutes wasted on the bus and the emptiness of his belly, he couldn't force himself to cross the road and open the door to the shop. He watched her for a minute, and then turned away, thinking of the empty eyes he had photographed and an image he constructed of the wet salty hair of naked women.

Infestation

1.

Smoke drifted slowly from the lazy red end of her cigarette and filled the afternoon with even more emptiness if that was at all possible. Traffic (a surprising amount for a Friday public holiday) concertinaed on the highway in front of her, sometimes fluent, sometimes stagnant, metallic boxes on wheels representing a whole series of lives continuing either with speed or in stuttering, jolting steps.

People's lives do continue though, she remembers again, always surprised when she remembers.

At one fifteen in the afternoon, her last break of the day, all elements of her immediate environment always managed to accentuate the numbness of her surroundings, even more so today because of the public holiday. A thick mid-September sun smears everything in her vision to just beneath a level of dull yellow while the constant train of droning vehicles refracts this dullness into all corners of her mind, predicting the long pointless roast that will be the summer months ahead. The poison smoke from her cigarette makes her drowsy and dull inside and out, so she stretches almost ninety degrees from her waist directly to her right to finish leaning on her elbow on the polished wood bench out the front of the hotel, eventually securing an image of languid defeated repose (though all her movements, the way she has always held all her body all the time, has always presented to her numerous observers a sort of sensual, available air, a fact more prevalent and deeply more arousing because of her complete unawareness of it). An unpleasant, inconsistent wind threads its way occasionally through the sparse gardening at the edges of the hotel car park, and the sheltered bus stops on either side of the highway (one with a smashed rear glass panel) remain empty and peeling in the arid early-afternoon sun.

The Comfort Inn, where Caitlin Maws works full-time as a maid and cleaner, is placed on a long thin stretch of land between the airport and the city, bordered on one side by a forgotten brown stretch of the river and on the other by a semi-heavy industrial area where they make carbon pencils and bent metalwork. The highway Caitlin now stares into or around or something runs between a line of hotels and the river, welcoming people home with a non-dramatic part of the world or whisking them away to holiday and pleasure, two concepts as alien to Caitlin as job satisfaction or, eventually, hope.

The Comfort Inn is one of many similar establishments in this forgotten stretch of perfunctory services, and all just as imaginatively titled – The Metro Inn, The Rest Hotel, Good Food Restaurant, The Bridge Service Station. These are not romantic destinations. They serve mostly interstate or international guests who visit the struggling city for a short time only, usually strictly business or troublesome stopover. There is the customary ceramic bowl of cheap bitter tasting tea and granulated coffee sachets for the guest at the hotels on arrival and an uneasy blend of weak grey and pastel pink décor that fumbles into a tangle of triangles and half-circles on the bedspreads and curtains in every room, a design that also often provides an uneasy backdrop to a number of Caitlin's thinner dreams. The tiny bathrooms in each apartment are cramped blue boxes and depending on the allocation of odd or even room number the view is either the highway out front or the dirty car park out back. It is a poor reminder for the many who see little else of the city.

Her break is nearly over. She still has the third floor to prepare, soaps to replace and shit to scrape off the inside walls of toilet bowls. She may watch a little daytime television in one of the far corner rooms and snatch a tiny bottle of whisky before she leaves, but already the rattling of the cleaning cart was knocking in her brain and flicking through her blood more convincingly than any small mercy she may gather from the repeated monotony of the afternoon. It was hot yes but there was an unpleasant coldness throughout her.

Caitlin stubbed out her cigarette in the messy grey sand in the pot plant provided and remembered again her great disappointment in realizing that even at the soulless pink prison of her work her mind was more relieved to be here than at the dark unnatural smear of her home.

2.

Every now and again he smelt it properly, the returning stench that clung to the bed sheets and the dark wood cupboard in the corner like caked mud or dried burnt beach sand. He sometimes correctly supposed it was himself, but that was the great advantage of being senile, or at least having the perception of what he believed were the first distractions of senility – he could comprehend any fact of oppressive immediacy into the diluted remembered haze of his past. The stench he sometimes guessed were the remnants of a congested swamp he had waded and pulsed through as a middle aged man in Singapore, or less likely the clinging of a cow pat he had accidentally fallen into as a very young child on a distant relative's farm in a distant childhood. He surmised all interpretations of the past were as relevant as the now and then remembered again not to care.

He saw no great wonder in being able to transpose his immediate environment like this. He saw and used it as a great trickery, giving him a power of personal translation or the insights of a witch. He felt the manipulation of time was a special form of relieving alchemy that was only defeated by the thick stench of his bedroom and the rough unwashed bed sheets clenched beneath his yellow horned fingernails. With all this skill and awareness, however, it could not stop him being anyone but himself.

He squinted down at the dust covered clock-radio at the side of his bed. The square digital red numbers stuck in the air like flat wounds. He knew they were fucking with him. Sometimes he was sure he had slept for almost the whole day and the clock displayed only forty minutes later. And other times, when he had just closed his eyes and opened them again, twelve hours were supposed to have passed by. He was convinced of it – they were changing the time on this stupid pissy little clock while he slept to mess with his already fragile mind. To manipulate the weak hatred and wield the tiny power they supposed they had over him in the only way they knew how.

'Quarter to three my arse', he retched through the crack of his drying throat, 'bullshit quarter to three!'

In the petty power game of the household he was and remained the witch king.

'I've got a full potty for you pricks to empty tonight,' he screeched into silent rooms, 'nothing solid there!'

He released his bitter grip slightly on the bed sheets after his outburst. His thin mottled chest heaved pathetically beneath his grey-blue singlet and he slumped slightly to the left against the smeared brown wall behind his head. The bedroom blind was drawn shut. If he had the want or the ability to calculate he would have realized the bedroom blind had been drawn shut for years. As he moved his left arm weakly on the covers a fine layer of dust puffed off the bed to infuse the room with a thicker, dirtier layer of smoke. He waved at some of it distractedly. If the clock was right (and who's to say it was) his daughter would be home soon and then he could complain with an audience. He had not let himself be washed for days because he had wanted to build up a crust.

He kept his eye focused on the thin yellow line created by his door being slightly ajar. He had kept the drawn blind company and had not been out of the room in years. He had no need to – decay was a symptom of life, but he still remembered the rooms of this house, the disarray and browning walls of the living room, the back end of the house where that angel of a grandson had cut his own entrance to his bedroom through the exterior as-bestos shell of the building, the dull purple kitchen with the greasy plastic table sunken into the rotting floor… and then on the meandering coat-tails of his thoughts it became all the rooms of all the houses he had ever lived in at other, less definite stages of his life. Shiny marbled bathroom floors and tidy kitchens ringing with the laconic spell of domestic harmony, cramped student dormitory's that slept four to a room and that smelt of promise, and then later, tiny bamboo shelters he had sheltered in on exciting, explor-atory research trips. The thin yellow opening to the rest of the house was the only window his unyielding mind needed for him to traipse through the sodden memories of his past life where he was always confronted with the irrefutable split that existed in the exact middle of his life. The first half and the second, the bright and the dark, the good and the unbearable.

And if it had been decided that his sinewy, thinned beyond despair body would not release him, then he would not allow himself to be the only one consumed by the stink. He would not let himself be the only one left in the dark. If his daughter would prolong his pain and pretend to suffer for it and if his grandson would challenge the strength of his witchery, then he had no choice but to destroy them both.

Even as his claws let loose their grip on the bed sheets and he slipped into a weakened sleep, the twist of his senility would not fully release him, for in his dream he still waded through the swamp of his room and always always the rancid taste of fur stuck deep in his throat.

3.

Around four thirty in the afternoon the distance between separate cars shortened and public transport bustled before and after each other in an-ticipation of peak hour. When five o'clock hit the traffic turned into one solid single metallic train and it was five or six changes of lights before an intersection was passed. Down from the Domestic Airport, along the North Western Highway, past the trashy cheap hotels where interstate guests oc-casionally spent a night and the rarely occupied boat sale yards remained empty, the highway passed beneath Tanning Bridge, the first major artery from the airport directly into the city. Underneath this block bland structure and stretching slightly back towards the airport, the tiny suburb of Tanning Bridge itself lay almost completely unnoticed by the passing throng of peak hour traffic. And, as a plant will fester and wilt through a lack of attention, so to did the suburb retreat itself of any importance it once may have had.

It had never been an area of any real opulence, but local councils had at least at one stage attempted to infuse it with a pulse. Cut off by the highway on one side, a dirty elbow of the river on the other and shadowed by the grey arch of the bridge above, both retail and domestic life had failed here. As it was a place never passed through to get to anywhere else, a constant revolution of stranger and stranger shops had inhabited the concrete boxes that stared listlessly out on to the highway. Grocers, bicycle shops, cane furniture, a tattoo parlour, even a hydroponic system point of sale, all had started with the true hope of success and all had folded within six months to a year. Now all of them, the whole souless complex that stretched along the empty hectic vein of North Western Highway, lay unpopulated and rotting, every second or third window smashed and scabs of paint peeling off the faded façades of the abandoned buildings.

There had been occasional promises of knocking the failed commercial venture down to create 'dynamic urban housing estates', but it was the absolute failure of past housing estates in Tanning Bridge that had stalled any real attempt at developing the rack of sunken businesses in the last five years. Going up and over the corrugated roofed shops there lay behind this desolate wall a widening scene of emptiness and banality, marked sporadically with abandoned household garages left open to the elements and deserted corner blocks used for the cultivation of thick, fuzzy weeds and dumping grounds for torn bald tyres. Shrill thin winds whipped off the brown river and flicked yellow grits of building sand from one empty block to the next. Incredibly, in a time of strong economic boom, housing prices here had dropped (one of only two suburbs in the entire metropolitan district to do so) and the few people who had bought into the soulless estates that had somehow been shoved together, quickly left, trying to stifle the impact of their financial loss and the psychological degradation such a place inspired in terms of quality of life. Street signs bent and faded through their utter lack of use.

Braydon Maws pushed through the fug of a late afternoon with the stalks of dead yellow weeds clutching at the frayed ends of his shapeless trousers. It was a strange time of day for him, a time to disperse outwards from himself between the two very real and sharp bookends of his work and his home. It was a good place to linger in his normally uncared for thoughts, there was never ever any one around to notice any splintered realizations that may suddenly strike too quickly or too deeply at his unguarded mind. It would have been difficult for a passive passer-by to notice any real change in Braydon at those moments of insight or disgust anyway. His walk was that of an introverted late teenager, head hung low into his widening chest with his uncomfortable hands occasionally brushing against the tops of the swaying yellow and green weeds. He never needed to take this longer path to his house from the bus stop, past the unfinished building sites and through the fighting gritty sand, but at least it delayed the inevitable. And besides, he enjoyed the feeling of his skin releasing and his name dispersing into the unused uncurbed roads of the suburb. It was a soothing disintegration into a very secret part of his day, released from the swings of judgment and the weight of presence. Sometimes he even managed to forget about his final destination, before the teeth of his grandfather and the brown walls of the corridor snapped his focus back into place and he heard once again the droning highway providing the endless soundtrack to his trudging path.

Turning left around a corner away from the river, Braydon glanced quickly up at his family home clinging on to the end of the road (hmmf, family, Braydon snuffed, and caught an edge of one of his long front forelocks of dark black hair in the corner of his mouth – the mess of his family did nothing to distil the weirder concept of it being somewhere somehow a normal idea). The house was one of only the few remaining that had been built in the initial attempts to found a community here, and the only one now inhabited. A few rangy rungs of wooden slats lifted the whole house about half a metre off the ground, though the one front step that helped you into the house had rotted away long ago (one of the weaker contributing reasons the house had 'trapped' Grandpa all those long years before). The house really did seem just to be holding on to itself and if caught at a particular angle, like the one Braydon had just snatched, there appeared to be a slight lean to it, like a weak-rooted tree being slowly pushed down a mountain. The decaying wood supports and green asbestos walls acted like an echo chamber and all and any noises made within the house bounced around the creaking foundations to create an atmosphere of a person whipped to be kept breathing. There were thick nodding weeds in the gutters and trilled green vein lines of damp underneath the faded white ceilings in the kitchen and the lounge room. It remained standing either because of the sodden infused pieces of furniture that clustered together ashamed of themselves in the dank corners of the house, or more, as Braydon believed, it stumbled along because of the unrelenting will of Grandpa's crooked finger.

About a year ago Braydon had cut a small and fractured door in a side wall of his bedroom that led directly outside, in to a fenceless backyard of yellow sand and a gritty low groundcover that spiraled outwards from the centre of its occasional roots. It was a month before his mother had noticed and by then there was nothing really she could do about it. It saved him the stinging shaft of that fucking damp brown corridor and the thin brown line of Grandpa's open bedroom door. He was proud of his renovation, with its crooked lines and gaps for sand and cockroaches to enter. He had cut it with a handsaw when his mother was out of the house. His grandfather screamed in a physical pain when he begun, providing Braydon with real stimulus and extra reason to finish it.

He pushed it open roughly now (he had to, edges still scraped together in its irregularity) and some thin green dust fell lightly down on to his head and shoulders. There was yelling in the house, mum was telling the old goat he would get dinner when he would get it. He heard his name being suddenly thrown about (Grandpa always knew the second Braydon entered the dwelling, the green walls of the house and the green skin of the man changed together accordingly during the different hours of the day). He slumped down on his thin single mattress, remaining in his supermarket work clothes, black pants white dirtied collared shirt, and snapped on some head phones. The crust of the house was creaking badly tonight. Only when the music was at its loudest, when it was thumping directly and rivetingly into his ears and skull, only then did he achieve the tiniest piece of alleviation and only then did the screaming green walls of his domestic environment recede slightly from the corners of his mind.

4.

When time is spent waiting or decaying for nothing in particular or maybe only the final end which he had begun to disbelieve in anyway (an end is sometimes a goodness) or even only another chance to release a hooked barb of his own misery into those closest to him, form and substance melted slowly together into a sliding, malleable presence of memory and environment. The thin crack from his slightly ajar bedroom door peering in to that fucking brown corridor often swung back and then away completely to admit people (intimate or thinly remembered) and with them complete separate locations or even whole years of his life. Occasionally he re-sifted through more pleasant fields of the few different lovers he had throughout his life, including his wife, a large, frowsy woman whose initial image of a young white canvas laying on her tummy in their first bed together and looking back at him with that intensely inviting air of compliance quickly dissolved into the terrified and cowering countenance throughout her whole face and body when the change stank through him. (Rarely did sparks or snapshots flicker in his head concerning the birth of his daughter, he no longer had the ability or morality to offer that fresh bursting parcel of life anything.) But mostly, almost constantly, like the edge of a small sharp sea shell caught beneath a toenail, there flickered through his head the mist of a humid afternoon, the descending green and dark green of a forest canopy, and the allure and surprise of a soft brown skin...

Grandpa's drowsing head shifted uncomfortably on the inconstant pillow. The sudden grimace etching across his mouth curled his fingers tighter on the sweating blankets.

He had been sent to Singapore as a construction advisor when he was in his mid-forties. Old Singapore was being razed to the ground. High density buildings were the way of the future, giant square pink and grey blocks speared on all sides by the raggedy steel poles of washing lines. They were willing and prepared to dominate the skyline and landscape. He was to oversee great slashing scars in the earth being transformed into concrete jungles. At home he had an adoring wife and a very young daughter. He was an ample bellied thick wristed Caucasian man sweating at the armpits and shouting instructions to anyone who would listen. He wore single coloured ties with short sleeved shirts and trained a thinning brush of combed brown hair over a broad head. He was a capable and solid man to have around.

On a rare afternoon off and on the advice of a fellow engineer who had been there longer than himself, he set out to find (as had often been romanticized to him since he arrived in the country) 'the old Singapore'. He quietly found himself sucking a small bag of coconut milk enjoying the gentle rhythm of a ramshackle boat slowly pushing its way through the lapping ocean water towards the tiny (undeveloped) island of Pulau Ubin, just north west of the mainland. A soft wind reflected off the water and soothed his humid brow.

In the dense ringing bush there was a sudden scattering rustle to the side of the dirt track... or perhaps it was coming from further to the left, or maybe above him and to the right. Then the bursting pack of black-faced monkeys that had been testing their feet on the leafy ground and on the branches of the trees were all around him, behind and to the side, in front and above. They swung through and alongside him with the chattering of teeth and the confident arcs of their long furry legs. He had hired a shaky bicycle at one of the few wood buildings that met the ferry on the shore, a few exhausted dogs raising their muzzles off the ground at his arrival. Two turns from the hire building and he was immersed in the dripping singing fingers of the forest. Before the monkeys he had passed the occasional dwelling hiding within the confident thick trees, hesitant sheds peering down from a small bank held together with chicken wire and guarded by discarded wooden crates and pots. The forest quickly re-consumed all though, releasing scurrying butterflies from within its climbing vines and echoing new and piercing bird calls from here or somewhere anywhere. The bike track sometimes curved towards a clay rinsed bay of the ocean before twisting back again into the leaf laden tangle.

(On his stinking bed Grandpa grimaced and kept arriving kept arriving always and always to this moment. The humid bush stunk in his bedroom.)

It was hot though. His shirt was wet through. He was off his bike and pushing over a rise in the track and drinking from a bottle of water he had bought at a sort of delicatessen where the boat had left him. On either side of him the forest was so thick he wondered how anybody had ever managed to forge a track through the midst of it.

And then stopped. Somewhere up to the right but further away and clouded in the trees he was aware of a dwelling but it floated more like a picture book or a painting, nothing tangible. He had interrupted someone evidently. In a small pool of an inland river, fed by falling watery hands over dark shaded rocks that dived and dribbled into the pool, a girl was washing. He had come upon her just as she slipped the thin straps of a green cotton dress over the light brown skin of her shoulders. Her hair was straight and dark. He was not that far from her. She was thirteen maybe, fourteen? The top half of her exposed, the man and girl were in stasis looking at each other.

He was a strong man with thick wrists and rounded shoulders. The insects of the forest shrilled with inspection. The thick air of the forest climbed through his head and stuck there, stuck forever. The rest of his life was an irrelevancy he had written before he had even thought of it.

5.

He had scrubbed his hands four times already but his palms were still sweating. It had always been a problem for Brownley, this sweating. No pale drab coloured business shirt could hide this condition and before he had even stepped a foot inside the office every morning his body was ringed with uneven orbs of moisture at every corner of his torso, the worst being the line of liquid that gathered and seeped through on top of the shelf of his rotund belly. He had the bellowing air conditioner on full blast but it was doing nothing to alleviate his current tension, possible only causing him to tremble a little more. He thought he may still vomit. He had been waiting two whole months, every day every second, for this soon to be moment. There was a chance, a strong chance, he may still wilt at the very final hurdle and not answer the knock on his hotel door when it came. He knew he might, but hoped beyond hope he wouldn't. There was a thick unpleasant knot that moved around knockingly to all four corners of his stomach.

Two months ago he really did not believe at all in any truth of the rumours. That was the only reason events had transpired as they did. If he had had any inclination about the absolute success and instant rapidity of activity that resulted from his unweighted question he would never have been able to go through with it – there was no strength of the daring in him. His stomach turned unpleasantly again just thinking about it.

Whenever anyone from the company travelled to this side of the country they were always put up at the Comfort Inn on the highway just down from the airport, and it was through Bruce Davison (by far and away the company loudmouth) that he first heard speak of it. There were four of them, four men, cramped into the small beige and cream kitchen area at work. Davison was pushing a sausage roll down the gullet of his mouth above a purple and red diagonally striped tie.

'Nah, I'm serious,' Davison sprouted, a rim of tomato sauce clinging to the left side of his mouth, 'if you get sent over there and you're away from your missus and all that, although it would be away from your right hand in your case, right Brownley?'

The two other men that had gathered in the fluorescent hole laughed quietly at their mates taunt. Brownley, the tauntee, remained silent, felt the sweat gather in the arse of his trousers.

'Yeah, all you have to do, there's this one particular maid… Catrina? Caitlin, doesn't matter, you'll know her cos she's the one that can suck start a leaf blower – '

Brownley was constantly amazed at this man's rank ease with himself and always wondered how in any way he could emulate it.

' – all you need to do, if you're willing to spend the extra cash, and why not hey, the room's free, is ask this one maid about the 'extra services' and bang, guilt free sex and company paid for cable man, a great weekend away.'

When Brownley himself was told he was going over for a week and also would be staying at the Comfort Inn this story only occasionally flickered at the back of his mind, such was the unlikeliness of any one of Davison's bullshit stories being true. It was only on the spark of recall that he heard himself asking about the 'extra services' when he eventually met Caitlin straightening his hotel bed on a dull Thursday afternoon. He had casually turned away for a glass of water and upon looking back the top half of her uniform was already around her waist and she was unfastening the grey straps of a thin bra behind her back. Brownley almost choked. She had released his large thighs before he could gather his thoughts and had the fat head of his penis rubbing over her parting lips before he could argue. It was the second time in his forty-two year old life that he had ever been with a woman.

On the droning flight home and all over the following droning months he could not stop thinking about her. The ride and slip of her back as she pulsed above him. When it became clear that he would not be sent back for work any time soon he took his holidays and booked a flight. He shut his ears to any disrespectful, smutty talk there may have been about her around the office. Similarly he himself did not talk of her. The last thing he needed was for those casual, often mocking, rarely polite work associates to know that he had fallen in love with a middle-aged hotel maid who performed any number of sexual acts with any number of clients to supplement her paltry income…

And now here he was, back in the room, the same room (he had made sure it was the same room), waiting to declare his intentions to a woman he barely knew. Just actually how he intended to do this was still a little unclear. He had brought her a present, a necklace of some misshapen pieces of stone, and had some idea about offering to take her away from all this, not that he was rich, or very handsome for that matter, he just… he didn't know. Allan Brownley, balding, large around the belly and thighs, and completely incapable of getting on top of the most reckless and spontaneous act of his life. He felt the sweat drip in the palms of his hands and in the folds of his neck. He was sure his armpits would be showing now. Out of pure comfort born of banal habit he had hung a white and blue tie over a light grey business shirt. He took his thin silver framed spectacles off and rubbed his brow.

I don't think I can do this, he thought. Now that it's here.

The knock came.

Outside Caitlin thought she heard a weak voice… then a cleared throat, before a louder 'come in' came to her. She pushed open the door with the requested extra towels underneath her arm.

He was standing at the end of the bed wiping his hands on his black stuffy trousers. The air conditioner was straining and blowing but she noticed wet marks at the corners of his arms. She smiled lightly and went into the bathroom to store the towels.

Ah fuck, he thought, fuck it hell, she doesn't even remember me.

He was still standing in the same position when she came out of the bathroom.

'Is there anything else you need?' she asked.

'You don't…' he stammered, 'I..' even his upper lip was sweating, she saw, 'I brought you a present.'

Any proof of her other life at this hotel Caitlin desperately tried to avoid, and it was only when she saw the large backside bumbling towards his suitcase that she remembered this man. A large, doughy rather damp experience that had left the man almost weeping at the end of a very quick encounter. She shivered for this very physical proof of a whole line of her life she tried to keep in the shadows.

'Look, I can't – '

'See, a necklace. It's… I got it for you…'

In his pudgy hands he was holding trembling a maroon coloured box stuffed with a garish stone necklace. She looked at it, to him, then back to the necklace.

'I don't know what this is mate, I don't know what you want but – '

He took a stuttering step forward.

'I want to see you. I want you to have this. I don't, I don't really – '

He wore a moustache of sweat as he teetered before her. It was impossible for her to believe.

'Then don't. Trust me, don't. It's very kind, I suppose, and all, but – '

'I guess, to be part of your life, is the thing, maybe, is what I want.'

The two people, who had been physically inside of each other, stood watching the sudden silence that lengthened between them. They could not have been further apart. Allan felt the knot in his stomach creep slowly painfully up into his throat.

'That,' Caitlin began, a steel wall, 'is the last thing you want. Go back to your nice business shirts. I can't… it's just better for both of us if you don't see me again.'

She turned and fled. The impersonal hotel door stamped itself shut behind her.

The jewelry case lay waiting on his thick hands. He was waiting for something else to happen maybe, something to explain to him what had just happened. The water at the edge of his eyes and his stuffed semi-erection pulled him in different opposing directions. Behind him the air conditioner blew itself solid.

6.

Maybe people were in the house. Maybe they were yelling at each other. Maybe he'd screech out himself to get some attention. Perhaps he already had – Caitlin was at the door.

'What is it dad?' she asked wearily.

He had not expected to get a reaction.

'Aw, I…' he spluttered, 'just wanted to know if anyone was around. Could have at least told me you were at home for Christ sake.'

'You were sleeping dad.'

'Big fucking shock. Never seen an old shoe sleep before? Not too hard to wake me up. Just use a rifle. That would wake us both up wouldn't it woman… Caitlin! Is that dropkick of a son of yours home? Is that who I can hear fucking fumbling around?'

Caitlin had slipped away from her father's door somewhere in the middle of this rant. He could continue on by himself now anyway. She often heard him berating on like this in his musty peeling room when she was at home. Her attitude towards it shifted between a great sadness and an intense distaste, like a mouthwash of bugs. She had tried listening to it for a time, slouched outside his bedroom with her head between her knees, hoping for an insight or indication into the murky unhappiness of his life, listening to the vitriolic tirade spewing out, speared with hatred and accusation, both personal and external. If she heard some of the hatred occasionally spent on her there was never any real indication as to why, and she remained attached to this dried stretched collection of skin and teeth (who incidentally happened also to be her father) like an old withered tree stump stuck in the messy ground searching for a place to grow. Hers was a thin shaky façade in accepting her life. It had become too unlikely and painful for her to truly recognize it and she did everything in her powers to never fully face it, a rare skill in her personal armoury.

Which is why she knew she had never truly broken through to her son. The hazed unclear image she had of herself must look like a nasty stain in his perception of her. She came back into their dark kitchen and saw him slumped on a chair where she had left him. Some of the thin stuffing on the kitchen chair he sat on had blurted out in ugly grey lumps. She wanted to display the love she had for this boy her son out on the table like a meal, a great Christmas meal with all the trimmings and sauces, but she knew she had not even the ability to walk to him and place a single hand on his head… she could not even remember what they were arguing about when her father had called her away.

'I worry about you, Bray.'

'Ah, the good old parenting fallback comment, hey mum?'

'Wouldn't know too much about that unfortunately, Bray.'

He was just coming to an age where he was beginning to realize his mother had more of the intelligence that longer life experience brings. The resentment this created in him swung equally between himself and her.

'You're always alone', the mother tried again, 'don't you have anyone your own age you could, I don't know – '

Braydon caught his mother's eyes deep in his own.

'What, bring them home to play?'

She knew. It was impossible. For the first time in ten, fifteen years perhaps a man had offered her a gift today (outside a few crumpled notes for a piece of arse, of course) and she had seen a dear intent in his eyes she could only just vaguely remember from some earlier time in her life. To be pulled in such opposite directions at that moment was a curious and unnatural feeling – her heart had leapt and sunk with equal force. Accept the gift, say thank you and then what? Reveal to him even the smallest piece of her grubby life? Try to relate to him even the strangest piece of her complete incomprehension with everything? Gritty crumbs crunched beneath her feet in the kitchen.

'I know' she replied.

Braydon looked up at his mother. He sometimes realized her occasional softness was a defeated one. Without any real hope, he thought he'd start the same conversation again.

'He doesn't have to stay here, mum,' he began.

From the bedroom a series a barks came, an animal calling out not to be

61

left alone. The evening descended another deeper shade of grey outside.

'Don't, Bray.'

'Can't you see mum? You must see. He's sweated himself into the walls, he's shat himself into the floorboards. This house stinks of him and it rubs into you like… like an oil or something, you know what I mean?'

Grandpa's bedroom was beginning to shake like the last carriage of a derailing train.

'Send him away, mum, send him the fuck away. You can do this!'

The bedroom was howling down and in upon itself and them, a gutted decaying beast.

'Please mum, for both our sakes.'

'Maybe…'

'Maybe what, maybe fucking what?'

'Maybe in some way I'm to blame for him, huh? Ever thought about that? I would have to be the one punished for my own life, wouldn't I?'

His mother's defeated weakness encompassed him. He didn't even know enough for his own life. He wouldn't let her see him cry.

'Pathetic, fucking useless,' he hissed as he shoved past her.

He was in such a rush to leave her, to get out of that brittle kitchen, he pushed his way into the brown corridor and not through his own room, the way he normally went. The crack into his Grandfathers bedroom suddenly cut across his eyes. It had been weeks since he had laid eyes on the old dragon.

He was waiting for him. His room had gathered its sticky tendons around the black pulse and left him dead centre. He pierced through the crack with split eyes into Braydon's innocent face.

'Love your mother do you boy? What a spike.'

He was a squeezing chest-bag with urine stained eyes.

'You'll be the death of me yet, kid.'

Braydon stumbled from the house into the whipping night air, stunned again at the seething vermin that lived behind his Grandfathers eyes.

To the distant echo of her father's shrill low repeated laughter, Caitlin looked nowhere around her into the brown dump of her retreating crumbly kitchen.

7.

Somewhere underneath all the layers of muck and unwashed sheets the semblance of purpose in his life had long ago been suffocated and slowly buried. Laughing at the tormenting of his family offered no release but instead created just another crusted layer of oppressive awareness about his inability to do anything about it. Only sometimes did he realize how much worse this made it, but that was only quick stabs underneath the turn of a blanket.

Fretting now on the gritty bed Grandpa again remembered that choice had been rightfully stripped away from him many years ago. That it was the lusted disregard of a young Singaporean girl's choice that had incurred the furred shadow into his life and body. That it was his choice to force on her what he had. And that finally, half a week after the first invasion and with a taste of sin on his lips he could just not seem to wash away, it was his choice also to be cycling through the humid air and tangled forests of the tiny island of Pulau Ubin, hoping to find her again.

He was dimly aware that he had lost his mind when he had stumbled across the girl washing herself in the forest and that the force of his body had followed his mind into a debased world it had not considered before. And for half a week his mind had remained dangerously unhinged as well, fumbling between astonishment and hunger, blind to its own atrocity. Finally, after hours of watching his colleague's mouths' move slowly and hypnotically somewhere in front of him and not understanding a single word that came out of them, he resolved to do something about it. He called in sick to work and, waiting on the warm humid wood pier for the little boat to take him back to the island, he found it impossible to sit still, and almost physically assaulted the captain who was waiting for enough passengers to make the short trip financially worthwhile.

The odd disregard the few fellow passengers gave him on the tilting ride to the island should have been some indication but he was blinded and in some ways possessed by an animal already. So he grimaced in his bedroom.

Only when he had scraped to a halt in a cloud of bicycle dust and insect song and found the pool empty, only then did he even consider the possibility that she may not be there. His horned feet kicked at themselves on his mattress. He let the bicycle fall through the humid air and looked wildly around. Somewhere he felt he knew he wasn't handling this very well. He felt his heart drop into his stomach and some sweat finger over his eyebrows.

Suddenly the dwelling away and up to the right that had last time been an abstraction to him, a mirage placed in an uncertain vision, came into focus. It revealed itself to be an unplanned collection of huts and houses, some wooden slatted walls with a tenuous link to the vertical and all of it grown up and around with the forest not against it. Windows were placed occasionally and unobtrusively like sleeping eyes.

This, surely, he felt or pleaded, would be where he would find her.

Thin bodied, sparsely feathered, desperate looking fowls scratched through the dust in the outer yard as he approached. Random wood poles connected with grey frayed cloth angled from the ground. He stumbled through discarded bottomless buckets and chipped wooden crates already as if possessed. And then like he had known (and in his present bed as he had tremulously feared) she was there, same green cotton dress, sweeping at the entrance of a shack standing alone by itself to the right of the main homestead. She ceased her movements on his splayed approach, caught his eyes, and softly, gently, maybe almost smiled. He felt as if the hair on his head was pulling itself out of its own ends as she slipped quickly through the dark rectangle doorway into the shack.

The old old man in the bed couldn't stand it, to relive over and over again this and always this moment every time he closed his eyes. He coldly remembered the irretrievable inevitable thumping of his feet on the gravel as he moved towards the hut, the internal screaming of rightful justice stabbing through his ears, destroyed by disgust, ruined by his own ruination.

There was a thin mist, almost a yellow vapor spread across the doorway and he could see nothing beyond it except the complete darkness. As he moved slowly through it his trance seemed to intensify as if now he could not even hear the sound of his own infrequent breathing. His arms and legs became soggy then inconceivably heavy before floating away from his senses completely. The doorway decreased and shut slowly behind him. He became aware of two figures between him and the door but was physically incapable of turning his head to see them. A small fire began to burn in the middle of the darkness, gradually illuminating a small area no bigger than a bedroom. The girl was nowhere to be seen and she would not be seen by him in the flesh ever again. There was a figure, though, seated behind the fire. This man or woman (it was impossible to tell, the wrinkled sacks of breasts belonged to either sex) sat cross legged behind the fire and wore the head dress of a feathered tiara, a central feather tall and thin and printed like the skin of a tiger. They wore nothing else except some poor cloth around their genitals and an ageless coat of wrinkles and dripping skin like that of melting bark. Occasionally the figure spoke in short indiscernible chants and in its raised right hand revolved a stone necklace that echoed in the room like the hiss of spitting.

He felt himself being moved into position on the other side of the fire. He found he was unable to give any resistance. He was seated in something like a flexed triangle, the two bulbous lines at his sides pointed towards the fire. The seated figure across the flames waved his hand underneath Grandpa's nose to emit more of the yellow mist which he inhaled deeply. His actions were not against his will because a will no longer existed. Some times the dense, suffocating heat of the room touched his skin but it was as if it was from many many miles away, like a planet he had heard of but never seen. He was wet through and unaware of it.

Then, across the ends of the fire, the ancient caught Grandpa's eyes with its own. They were white and cloudy, a sink of time and distance. Despite the desire to scream the intruder could not emit a whimper. The figure slowly began to chant louder and deeper, trapping the intruder within the white cloud of his face. He produced a cage from behind himself in which a creature shitted and gnawed at the cane bars of its imprisonment. It revealed itself to be a rat the size of a small cat, yellow teeth and black eyes and on parts of its dark fur white hair that had matted into spikes. The fire and the rat hissed at each other with equal fear.

From behind Grandpa's arms were clasped and his jaw was thrust open. Finally he found some struggle in his body but it was too late. The terrifying old figure behind the fire had the seething animal in his hands and was leading the snout of it towards Grandpa's open mouth. The rancid spit of the animal dropped on his tongue, and then its rough, dirtied whiskers was on his lips and in between his teeth. It felt like his jaw had unhitched itself from his head and kept opening wider and wider to receive the filth. The whole head and two front claws of the thing were now inside him, fighting against the confines of his shredding throat. The old creature feeding the rat into him was now booming their chant. Unable to breath, vomit, scream, the rat continued to disappear down Grandpa's throat, the shit underneath its back claws and the spike of its tail. Ripping out one last screech of its chant, the trembling figure closed Grandpa's jaw with the heel of their hand and Grandpa uncontrollably, and deeply, swallowed.

And then he is running, surging through the swamps of Pulau Ubin, retching, hacking, infused throughout his entire wrecked body with fur and teeth. He tries endlessly to vomit, to hack something out of the filth of his stomach or the dirt out of his lungs but only produces small clumps of greenish yellow bile. He lies in the pools of his own sick, crying swamps and being devoured by relentless insects, knowing already that it is too late. When he swallowed he felt the animal disperse into all parts of himself up to his skin, infected and forever more stung with vermin. He retches, belches, but can only crawl through the mud and over his bed and down the disease of his own creation.

8.

Becoming more accustomed and able to spend an entire night outside and on the street was of no real consolation to Braydon. His satisfaction of returning home in the morning and frustrating his mother by not answering her frenzied questions about where he had been all night was tempered by an awareness of some form of decline, a displaced emotion of a goal achieved yet never desired. He had only so far spent a handful of nights on the street, and though the length of the night's emptiness was becoming less of a shock to him there was some form of the increasing taste of the actual street in his mouth every time he found himself trudging back over the empty sandy blocks to the poor lopsided house that had been his childhood home and also, of course, home and holder to the witch.

There was always the strangest daze that spread gradually over him on a night outside. He rarely slept, maybe only fitfully at bus shelters. On the first few nights he had spent vacant time lingering and waiting outside the small city supermarket where he stocked shelves. He drifted there probably from a thin sense of association and recognition but carelessly one night he had fallen asleep outside the store and was almost recognized by a fellow employee beginning their days work early one morning. He slipped quickly away with the dirt beneath his eyes pricking at his reddening face.

There was a girl at the store he had to some degree connected with. She had sometimes guessed at this silent young man's other darkening life but was yet to know any particulars. She had even offered him a room for a while if he needed it. For an instant upon offering the room she saw a deep release flow from Braydon's widening green eyes and a shadow lift just so slightly from his face, before he retreated again, turned his head, and quietly said no. How could he tell this girl, Laura, with her tight brown ringlets and simple glasses, anything of his life, and more importantly, how could he ever in his life leave his fucking mother.

She flickered through his mind especially this night. It was colder, much colder than any of the other nights he had spent outside. There was the faint tang and promise of approaching rain in the deadening air and underneath the silent street lights. He walked briskly, but nowhere, slapping his cold sides with his hands. Any attempt he had ever made to convince her to leave that house had been quickly diverted. She spoke of a man Braydon could not even begin to conceive let alone recognize in that shriveled capsule of a barely living thing. She spoke of a generous, interested father who had supported all her decisions and dreams and who, incredibly, had made her laugh. She spoke of an untangled honest love that had been reciprocated fully between a father and a daughter.

But rarely, occasionally, she sometimes spoke of a change that had overcome the man after an overseas trip cut rapidly short. She had said after she and her mother picked him up from the airport he had not said a single word on the drive home but instead remained doubled up in the passenger seat, constantly spitting into a handkerchief. She spoke of a man who was suddenly vicious and cruel and relentless, a viper. She spoke of a power that gave this new man a strength and an evilness she could not have before imagined, so even as his body dramatically withered in front of her eyes it also stretched and hardened like the impenetrable stinking crust of a baking salt lake. She spoke of a terror and a confusion he made her feel somehow responsible for, and of a sickening burden she felt intrinsically and hopelessly enslaved by.

In short, she spoke of two different men, one of which Braydon had never seen and could not believe in. Braydon was not stupid, and he knew all the doubts he had about himself, all the tension that existed between himself and his mother, and all the stink he smelt during his waking hours, no matter where he was… all was due to one horned old wrinkle with hatred written indelibly on his skin. Yet try as he might, he felt he was powerless to do anything about it. More and more he was beginning to realize he could do nothing to save his mother.

Turning a blank corner an unusual yowling came to his ears. The street was empty save for the occasional blue night light that eased out of closed barred shops, yet halfway down the road a small shape struggled. It rocked and swayed, a distressed outline the same damp colour as the surrounding night. Coming closer Braydon realized it was a dog, a grey and black matted mongrel that had a leg trapped in a broken street drain. It had fallen in such a way that by trying to drag its back right leg free, it only resulted in impaling itself further. The dog was clearly frightened, and in pain, and in between yelping it snapped at Braydon's approaching hands. He spoke to it softly, slowly, let it smell the back of his hands, before he rubbed its ears. It was all whimpering now, stuck in its poor fear. It had calmed its struggling slightly in between its sad yowling, and Braydon slid his hand down just below where it had been caught and carefully pulled it free.

The dog instantly hopped clear in some clearly painful circles, rapidly bent and licked at its wound, then hobbled off and away down the street as quickly as its injured leg would allow it. The night engulfed the animal back into itself and only the empty street remained.

A light shower began. Braydon remained motionless underneath the sure cloak of the rain, watching where the dog had disappeared into the darkness. The bitumen soon shone with a thin sheen of water, and the cold corners of buildings dripped their fingers on to the garbage below.

Braydon was finding it difficult to move. He began to realize that nothing actually was stopping him accepting Laura's offer of a room to live in, that in fact it could possibly be the simplest and easiest thing he had ever done. He was wet through already, wet as the rain itself. All he had to do was walk through the rain and the sunrise to that house one last time, pick up some clothes and a few regardless objects and leave through the door he had made for himself at the back of his room. He saw it, the door, left hanging open in the morning, dust and sand moving in and out of the doorway like he had never even been there. There was not one thing stopping him.

The rain tasted like some form of clear acid on his tongue, cleansing his mouth of his teeth and his thoughts. It ran over and through him like a bath, leaving him clear, hollow and able. Braydon moved away, sensing only the fire inside him that was ignited by the rain and the definitive promise of a morning.

9.

The taxi pulled quietly away in the early morning light. Around him the empty sandy blocks lay flat upon themselves in the yellow windless air. There was a hum and a growl of congested traffic in the distance. It looked as if one irrelevant push on a corner of the house would topple the whole thing over. Vicious weeds struggled between the sizeable cracks in the brick-red path leading to the front verandah.

Can this really be the place? he thought, already damp beneath the arm-pits.

Allan Brownley had almost packed his meager suitcase and left after his failed attempt of presenting his gift to Caitlin. He surmised it had gone about as bad and as embarrassing as he had expected it would. But he had remained, and decided that if he had gone this far he may as well fuck it up completely.

The hotel attendant behind the front desk said it was completely against company policy and illegal besides to give out an employee's home ad-dress' to unrelated hotel patrons and that there was nothing at all he could do to help him. Soon after there was a knock at his door. It was a maid and, though Allan had not seen her at all, she had apparently overheard the whole conversation with the attendant and was more than happy to divulge Caitlin's private information to him, especially if there was a small fee involved.

'Say... fifty bucks?'

'Fine,' he blurted out immediately.

'Crap. I could have asked for anything, couldn't I?'

He ended up paying her a hundred dollars for the address, and to also avoid any more sly, knowing looks than was necessary.

It was early early Sunday morning. Allan could not wait in that hotel room (complete with the sting of good and bad memories) any longer. The sun was little way above the horizon and the day was clear and sharp with the promise of heat later. There was not a breath of wind. The house seemed uncomfortably quiet aside from a low inconsistent croaking that could have been the wood work trying to hold itself together. Allan's re-solve was a weak one but he persevered, feeling the crunch of weeds be-neath his tentative feet.

The groaning of the floorboards on the verandah underneath his weight cracked loud enough to wake the whole morning let alone the immedi-ate occupants of the dwelling... but still nothing in the house stirred. The croaking that Allan had heard earlier, a painful, interrupted slur, continued. The front door was half open. Allan felt more and more convinced he was at the wrong house and that the taxi had brought him simply to a decrepit shell long since abandoned. Adjusting his eyes from the bright yellow light of the morning he poked his head around the door and found himself looking down a long brown corridor. There was a thick smell like that of a rabbit hutch and at different spots on the floor discarded lumps of clothes lay beaten against each other in random unwashed piles. A dusty uneven side table lay hidden against a corner of the wall with one and a half pair of shoes strewn across its face.

'Hello?' tried Allan, a little more confident than he may normally have been because of his assumed lack of response.

The low intermittent croaking abruptly ceased. Allan had not considered it to possess a human element. He listened. He could not now decide whether it was more silent inside or outside the house. He tried again.

'Hello?'

The response came as a forced hiss, spreading throughout the quiet air before him.

'Come… here.'

The front door was only slightly ajar so Allan had to push through with his belly to enter the house. His white shirt became a little smeared at the contact. At each hesitant step along the corridor the tired boards creaked so painfully Allan felt sure he was about to lose a foot through one of them.

'Hello? I – '

'Yes, yes…'

The hissing came through a gap past a scratched frayed edge of a door on the right hand side of the corridor. Allan edged his way cautiously towards it. For the first time he wondered at the prospect of Caitlin having a man in her life. He still wondered if this was even the right place. Regardless of the outcome he needed an answer now.

Whatever he had expected to see it could never possibly have been this. The old (an insufficient word) old man was terrifying. He was sitting up on a thin mattress, round piercing eyes gleaming out of a putrid starved face devoid of all muscle and health. He gripped a dirty blue blanket with the horns of his hands. The top lip was drawn back over his teeth like an animal in pain and the gaps between his missing teeth were filled with rotten shards of dirty yellow. A fist released his chest to breathe in and out in shuddered bursts and a deteriorated tongue lolled around the hole of his mouth. The hutch smell intensified around Brownley's nostrils.

'God, sorry…', Allan stammered, gripping the door frame, 'I… couldn't,… Caitlin?'

To his great surprise the old lizard began to curiously nod his head.

'This is where Caitlin lives?' Allan asked.

The old man nodded as he leant back against the mank of four or five previously yellow pillows. Even that small effort seemed to knock the last strands of strength out of the old creature's chest. With the crooked bone wrapped in the skin of the right index finger the decrepit old man beckoned Allan to come closer.

Allan sidled into the room. The animal stink was almost overpowering. It seemed that the only thing that had moved in the room for years was the wheezing fossil on the bed. All other furniture items in the room were coated with a greasy layer of dust and disregard. It was difficult to distinguish outlines on the corners of the room. Human fecal matter clung to the corners of all things solid and material.

The ancient man beckoned Allan closer still. He noticed one or two thick white bristles sticking into or out of the relics withered chin. Allan bent down through the stink.

'Caitlin?' spat the old man.

Allan nodded. The old chest on the bed heaved itself as it prepared to speak again.

'What do you want with that fucking little slut?'

For a moment it felt to Caitlin like the hysteria that had been clawing at the edges of her life had finally taken total control and was making her see things that were not there. The rotund bum that was obscuring the view of her father seemed to belong to the poor man (Allan, she had remembered) who had failed to deliver his gift to her the afternoon before… but how was that possible? No part of her life either at the hotel or at this house had ever crossed into the other, and this had not been an accident. She felt if they had it would be like seeing yourself in the future, before the resultant and devastating implosion.

The most alarming provocation of her hallucination was of an unfamiliar pleasure in seeing him standing there, right there, in her house.

'Allan?'

The large figure of the man did not disperse into fantastical dust but instead straightened and turned at the mention of his clearly real name. Caitlin felt an incredulous, unexpected curl at the edge of her lips as she watched the spectacled eyes of this man dissolve from something near horror to a spark of great joy upon seeing her.

'Caitlin', Allan beamed, 'I… I came to find you.'

Caitlin knew she was not allowed to feel these feelings.

'I see.' She tried to sound nonplussed, but in the end could not contain a smile.

Then he was on him. With a guttural snarl or a rip in the air Grandpa had sprung from his mattress and latched himself on to the back of the intruder. Allan felt the jagged ripped claws of the old man's hands and feet rip into his flesh with an unexpected strength. The human animal bit down savagely with his few remaining teeth into the soft exposed side of Allan's neck. Blood streamed freely. Caitlin screamed.

Braydon was walking back to that swollen house with his strengthened resolve in the clear light of a Sunday morning for the last ever time. A short while before a silent taxi had passed him, unusual in itself for this area but especially strange for this time of day. Approaching the teetering fucking house he suddenly heard the air tear apart and then his mother scream. Running over the few empty blocks before the house he almost unconsciously picked up a metre long metal pole abandoned in the sand.

Entering in to the brown hole of his Grandfather's room he saw a man he had never seen before staggering under the claws of his Grandfather's raging attack. His Grandfather's face and one whole side of the man's white shirt was dank and red with blood. The large man was flailing uselessly at the animal on his back with weakening, ineffectual arms.

Caitlin and Braydon caught each others eyes. Caitlin saw the steel pole in her son's hands. Braydon saw the distraught, maniacal terror in his mother's ruined face.

'Do it Braydon!', she screamed and cried, 'for the love of Christ, DO IT!'

Braydon swung the pole in a clean, wide maddening arc through the room and over the years of his and his mother's torment and collected the venomous old man flat on his withered old brow. He fell back on his bed with a sodden thump. Allan fell to his knees, blood streaming through his fingers at his neck.

Mother and son looked down at the seething, writhing thing gasping on the bed. There was a clear straight break across his forehead. As he spoke he spat blood and teeth out on to his own chin and neck.

'Fucking… stupid… cunts… … wasn't… my fault…'

The old man crackled on the mattress. Braydon raised the bar above his head, and brought it thickly, and finally, down.

Allan wiped his eyes with his free hand as he tried to regain his breath and focus. He struggled to his feet just in time to see Caitlin pull a dirty sheet over a creature on the bed. It was a large, misshapen rat with matted white stripes running down the hump of its back. It yellow eyes were still and its broken snout gristled with blood.

10.

On an empty block down near a forgotten elbow of the river the haze of late evening was being thickened by the grey fumes of a small fire. There was the rancid smell of burning damp fur in the air. Close by, a mother and son stood watching the fire, the taller boy with an arm around his mother's shoulders. Further behind in the yellow grey haze a frumpish man with a bandaged neck also stood watching.

The small fire leapt in and over itself and took its time. If ever it wilted the young man poked and turned it so it sparked again. They would let it burn as long as it needed to, until it was spent and light and gone. Above them the grey smoke of the fire fought against itself for a time before eventually relenting to the greater stretch of the sky and dispersing into an irrelevant, useless nothing.

Death Scenes

You should see me astride the stage, taking leave of my senses, electrified by the opiate of performance. The apotheosis of Richard Milton, mouth trembling, alight with rage and pity and greatness. A lungful of air passes through my teeth, over the perfect symmetry of rounded vowels: *I have not fallen, but I am destroyed.* You can feel the charge on my skin, the other man in my eyes, summoned from the guts, alive only in the costume and deception of portrayal. My hands move through the air with dramatic gestures, coming to rest on the cool flesh of her arm.

Only then do I see her through the paste of stage make-up. Only then do I see her eyes, at that moment when I should be immune. At the precise instant of my character's death.

And then, many years later, to be astride a deathbed where everything is acting and nothing.

The Director starts up from the darkness beyond the stage. Lights flare into brightness, I see the receding gloom of his brow, aware of the decomposing character within me, that temporary death I feel twenty times a day.

No, no, no. Richard, I'll tell you again and again until you do it right. I leap to my feet, everything traduced into the minor death with which he disagrees. *You are surprised, not saddened. You maintain your anger, just as you realise you are dying, you are dead.* The Director strikes his hands together. *Just like that.*

My hands rest on her arms and she comes closer. I cannot stop the surge of longing as she comes. I feel the flush of my throat as her mouth opens on mine, as her arms throw off my hands and her hands travel around my waist, from the back to the front, brushing across. They have cropped her hair and painted her lips dark red. I do not see the knife as it plunges into me, but I am aware, somewhere in that part of me that is real. I look down, surprised, trying to push her away. Her eyes are transformed. I sense laughter in them. I begin to see the darkness.

I have not fallen, I begin, but pause, resting my hand against the wall behind me. I cannot move away from her. Her face follows me as I disappear.

No, No. The Director. Why did you pause? *Only for a breath. Only for a last breath.*

I have not fallen, I say, drawing a hard breath, *but I am destroyed*. Then the absence of light. I come as close as I can to my own demise, imagining my own naked corpse, imagining that final hour tattooed with all the faces I can remember. I come close to death without dying, sensing its rigor mortis filtering through my wrists and its bloodless lips on my throat. As my eyes close I see all these things, astride the stage, beneath columns of light and her immutable stare.

Then the applause. I open my eyes and see that she is pleased with the brutal imitation I have made of another man's death. The Director applauds slowly. Yes, yes, he says. But I am not all alive, there is something of me still behind those heavy curtains, the look of her that I carried with me, whatever it was stirring in her eyes, that part of her that I thought was not acted.

I wait outside the stage door for her to appear, brushing my hands against my hips which are like a woman's and of which I am ashamed. The Director asked me to disrobe for a scene, but I refused. In my mind I would see only her, awash in the white glaze of my skin. How would she have seen me? Could she have uncovered the death that I carry in my heart? She would have seen me as I was, a worn out case, carrying the longing for her in my empty hands.

The stage door opens and she greets me, leaning into me, still smelling the pleasure of the rehearsal.

Brilliant, she says. *I almost cried watching you die in there*. Her face flushes with the cold and she pulls her coat tighter.

I think I almost did die in there. There is nothing that can stop me. I had seen her for the first time, closer than I had ever seen anyone before. I knew already every part of her. I can see behind her skin. So I reach out my hand and touch her face, resting my fingers on her lips that still carry traces of paint; dark scratches in the yellow light of the street lamp.

But it's only acting, she says, removing my hand from her face, still holding it, but in an empty and distant way.

I realise that she does not feel every word she utters on stage, she cannot feel them rising within her with the rehearsed surprise of their revelation. Nothing to me is acting. I am the characters I become and nothing less. I am alive with the animation of another man. Desire plates my skin in perspiration when she comes near, when her lips touch my lips. I do not need to act the surprise when the longing is destroyed with the thrust of her hand, but I am consumed with the revelation of her hatred and then what I can make of my own death. I see the resumption of darkness, the contempt formed by the muscles below her eyes. Then the flare of light on the other side of the fallen curtain. The death I die over and over, every night, twenty times a day.

And so the season begins, night after night for four weeks. I enter the stage time and time again, repeating every movement, every phrase as though nothing had been rehearsed. I furrow my brow where the script requires it to be furrowed, hold my head in my hands after the words that lead me to despair have left her mouth. Every night the roundness of my waist feels the passing of her hands for the first time.

No sooner than my head comes to rest against the rough old mattress, no sooner than my eyes close on the nocturnal shapes of the bedroom's ceiling, do I conjure from my thoughts the angles in her face, the crooked lines that seemed to converge on me as her hand thrust in the knife. Again, I feel the weight she puts into it, her breath that I can taste in the meeting of our mouths.

I do not act when I fear she is alive within me, another character who refuses to die, and who knows the arrangement of my own death.

Then I fall asleep. I dream of the stage, the black mouth opening out before it in which the invisible audience fold and unfold their arms. I see them as types of black in the blackness. It's a dream from which I have never woken. I open my eyes and find myself once more astride the stage, delirious with the men who possess me; I utter the words, weep with their tears and feel the terror that travels through their veins.

And, on stage at this moment, I speak the words that could have come from me. I hear them ring above the hundred heads with the clarity of a bell.

What else is there to remember?

At this age everything is acting, everything is pretence, even the memories that come at you like steam from a pot. A thousand times I've watched the shadow play on the wall. I cannot tell her, I cannot speak to the memory of her. Days and weeks are laid out in a path leading around her and around again.

The Director looms above me, testing the mettle of his trimmed beard by trying to pluck out its hairs. His hair is still dark. He is as I remember him, but out of focus. She is there, but I cannot see her, somewhere in the periphery, always expecting to be found, but never seen.

The lengths of the pauses in his speech have not been mitigated by the years. He still thinks out every sentence before it passes his lips. *Milton, that's not what we wanted. He's lying on his deathbed, the sheet drawn up to his chin. A longer pause. The weight of so many years sits on his chest. The actress is gone, but he has not forgotten her. He imagines that he can see her.*

All at once, I know it. I see how to bring it to life. Interminable sorrow. Undying light that draws her face into the field of focus, she is the same woman she always was, sharp features softened with stage make-up. The arcs of her eyes converge on me, who does not see her except through the mouth of my despair, though I cannot see her and the lights flare into a white sheet and I speak the line, words through the machine gun of my

throat, my hand is a stage also, brought to your face where you misunder-
stand, where you can't understand, where everything is acting but nothing
also   where every hand is lunacy
    she is here but she is not here   then for an instant I see my-
self   then nothing

The Park

One warm summer afternoon Lee ran out the front door and down the three front steps of her house. As she ran her pink and white sandals smacked themselves against the red concrete path stretching down over the front of her garden. On either side of her uncut grass and overgrown weeds buzzed in the early afternoon sun. The thick red heads of bottlebrushes further down the path rounded with complacency while bees edged around them before landing on their pungent, outstretched fingers. A thin wooden letterbox slept in the sun and as Lee passed it she gave it a gentle pat on its head like an old family pet. She skipped up on to the sandy verge at the edge of their property and waited, checking both ways.

Lee was going to the park across the road from her house. Mum had said it was okay, and she always went across to the park around this time anyway, especially during school holidays. Lee loved the park. It stretched over a large open area and in the warm afternoons when the easterlies blew and blurred everything all together Lee could sometimes feel herself disperse across and apart like the wind and almost disappear completely to herself. Pieces of old faded playground equipment lay scattered around the black brown trunks of trees and the ground was a mesh of cooch grass and sand. Around the base of the trees the grass gave way completely and rings of dry grey sand surrounded the thick trunks. In the green pieces of leaves above which rattled and clapped when the easterlies blew butcherbirds clucked and fought while from within the mix magpies called and cajoled to each other. Lee and her mother lived far away from the city, in an outer suburb that was quiet and slow. Most days Lee had the park entirely to herself, and she would roam and skip through the trees for hours, following invisible paths in her mind until the sun began to sink below the rooves of the houses on the west side. Then Mum would come looking for her, and guide her home gently into the bright warm life of their kitchen where the familiar enticing smell of dinner lay waiting for her.

Today Lee skipped across the road, her short white one-piece dress fluttering against her legs in time with a gentle breeze. She hopped over the circular pine fencing that surrounded the oval. She ran a few excited steps and instantly had some dry hot sand stuck between her feet and her sandals. She hated that, especially when her feet started to sweat, but she knew there was nothing she could do about it until she went home and took her shoes off at the front door. Still, she was away now and the heat of the day came to her in waves. Free in her park Lee already sensed her thoughts drift down into her body and into her walk as she began again to think with her fingers and speak with her skin. Her irrelevant hair played by itself around the gentle arc of her face. She began to follow an imaginary trail she sees in the sand in wide sudden loops and lazy white limbs. The arms of the sun soothe and release her and in different places around her bounce off the long black feathers of willy wagtails. A beige car passes in the distance, old and dirty and seemingly without any noise. For the moment there is only here and the sun and the dry grey sand that speaks of time and waiting. Without the weight of decision Lee glides over to a set of swings and sits down in one, watching the curve of the gentle world revolve beneath her.

As the swing moved easily through the air Lee trailed patterns in the sand with her feet. She rested her head against the thick old chains of the cradle. She was dreaming about what Mum might cook for dinner tonight and when she would see Aunt Sal next when she looked up and saw a boy dressed in a black t-shirt and blue shorts move away from her towards a turnstile ride. He jumped on and pushed himself around with his right leg, looking over at Lee every time he spun around in her direction. He had short-cropped blonde hair and wore black sneakers with white socks. Every time he pushed off the ground for more speed a puff of sand blew up at his feet. Lee looked away, back down toward the ground. She didn't care about any boy.

When next she looked up he was closer, watching her from behind a tree. The turnstile ride spun silently and slowly by itself behind him. Lee poked her tongue out at him. He gave her the finger. He was probably a couple of years older than her, eight maybe, or nine. He had full, chubby cheeks and wide blue eyes. He moved around to the front of the tree and rested against it with both hands behind his back. He kicked at the sand in front of him.

'Go away!' shouted Lee, her brown shoulder length curls sweeping across her face.

'Don't want to,' said the boy, staying by the tree.

Lee looked back down to the ground but felt the strange boy's eyes still watching her. She heard his heavy footsteps crunch over the dead and dying bracken littered across the ground between them.

'I could tell my mum on you! I just live over there.'

'What for?' said the boy, moving in to hang off the swings rusted metal frame, 'I haven't done nothing.'

Lee noticed mottled freckles stretch all the way up his exposed forearms.

He swung on the frame at an angle and let his knees bend.

'Want to see something?' he said, arms outstretched and brash. In the background the turnstile ride finally creaked to a slow, jolting halt.

'What?'

'I'm not gunna tell you, you gotta come and see it.'

Lee followed the boy who for a little while walked backwards so as he could still face her. Behind her the abandoned swing jumped around on the end of its chains as if whistling or calling her back.

On the far side of the park directly in line with Lee's house the playground area tangled up into thicker scrubland punctuated with clumps and clusters of paper-bark trees. High grasses and weeds grew around the bases of the paper-barks and a thick wiry bush fought in and over itself along the ground. Lee didn't like to play on this side of the park very much. She saw a few of the older kids over here sometimes and the thick ugly undergrowth could scratch at your skin or rip at your dress if you went too near it.

Still, also, she knew she was almost seven and this boy didn't worry her too much, he was just a dumb boy with scabs on his knees like all the others.

'What is it?' Lee asked again, fiddling with the hem of her dress.

'It's over here,' said the boy, pointing to the scrubland, 'you have to come and see it over here.'

The grass in the scrubland was thicker and Lee's small feet sunk deeper into it than on the struggling cooch grass in the middle of the park. The air sounded louder here too, half stripped layers of paper-bark beckoned off their trunks and dirty bare twigs stretched themselves down from the branches. The boy skipped ahead, stumbling on the unseen debris in the undergrowth. He bounced off the edge of a paper-bark while Lee stumbled on behind him. There were more flies here too and they were fatter and hungrier, they stuck on your nose and your eyes and crawled around your face even when you tried to shoo them away. Heat alternated between the shadows and there was the dry grey taste of sand in your mouth, an early reminder of the long dry summer ahead.

On the decline of a small embankment the boy crouched behind a shape on the grass. Lee had definitely decided she didn't like this part of the park. She approached cautiously now, the blades and heads of weeds slashing at the skin of her small white legs.

'Look,' said the boy over the shape. Lee looked. At first she couldn't tell what it was, there were so many flies.

'It followed me in here. I dunno whose it was.'

The four poor legs were very still and lifeless. Half its face was missing and an eyeball hung by a white strand over the dog's mouth. Through a crack in the skull brown lumps of brain had begun to dry in the sun.

'Then it just lay down and I picked up a rock and just started bashing it,' said the boy breathlessly, looking quickly up at Lee. She saw now he was actually very scared, his shoulders tight and his eyes wide and open. She hadn't noticed before but the ends of his fingers and his knuckles were stained a faded red.

'I just, I just kept bashing it, and bashing it...' said the boy, touching the lifeless dog with his foot.

Lee turned and ran. For a while in the thick grass she felt like she was getting nowhere, that her legs were just going up and down on the spot, not moving an inch, but then she broke through the scrub and sped across the open floor. The black trunks of trees and the hulks of playground equipment threw up obstacles where before there had just been open space, she had to pick her way through the maze. Only once did she allow herself a quick look back. She saw the figure of the boy racing away through the paper-barks in the opposite direction. Leaves and light and the strangled calls of magpies flashed all around her as she ran, the park swallowed up behind and chased her.

When she reached the road she didn't even stop to look she just ran straight across it and up and over the front path before pelting her way through the front door without even taking her shoes off. She found mum out the back hanging up the washing. She cannoned into her legs hanging on to just below her mum's shorts. She grabbed on and felt warm tears spread down and over her mum's skin.

'Baby, baby, what's the matter honey?'

Lee just hung on, feeling the reassuring hand brush slowly across her hair. It was hot out the back. On the line the washing hung heavy and flapped about like broken birds. In her mind Lee heard the click of grasshoppers and was nearly sick thinking about their thin, brittle legs.

The Short Life of Rodney Small

Nineteen forty eight

We had been clearing bush when we found it – stiff and blue, face down. I reckoned he'd been done in, but when I called Dad (I called out 'Da, Da, look 'ere, look at him, he's been done in…') he poked it in the ribs and shook his head: "E's done in alright and I reckon he done himself in.' He was face down, just off the track that had been trodden around the estuary before circling the water and then bending up towards Tim's Thicket. We'd been clearing trees in the north and I was riding between the streams and the track when I found him.

Dad said, 'Poor bastard. See the gun there?' You could see the steel through the mud. The body had contorted around itself, limbs bent around in the way that dead ones do. He was belly down in the mud, with muddy leaves pushed up over his head and his gear missing. Dad said it looked like he had been interfered with, poor bastard. Maybe someone else had found him and worked him over for his wallet; there was nothing on him to say who he was, not even a watch, not even a shred of his shirt.

'Recognise him?' asked Dad. I shook my head. His hair was cropped, probably another poor bastard soldier – got back and can't to make a go of it. 'Jesus, He's lost an arm.' Dad had a poke and we saw that it had been lost for some time. 'It's a stump. Someone must know him from that.'

Eddy had heard me yelling out for Dad and he pulled up around the track. He limped, but quickly, to get there in time to see whatever it was. He dragged his lame foot through the mud. Eddy had red hair thinning on his head and more bristling on his chin and his chops. He laughed because he wasn't as bright as the rest of us – didn't figure out what he was seeing. He'd seen enough living things die, but sniggered at this poor bastard with the mud caked up on him as if he'd been lying there in the dirt forever with the leaves swirling around him. Sometimes you'd want to smack Eddy in his wide-open mouth and dirty teeth for laughing at things he bloody well shouldn't have been laughing at. Dad told him to shut his fuckin' mouth.

I rode back to call the copper while Eddy grinned and Dad searched around, poking sticks into the leaves and turning over the bushes near the body. The shade grew darker as I galloped down the tracks, dirt splaying up behind me, smelling the sweat of the horse, gripping his ribs because the saddle had become loose. I slipped off him in the yard and Mum grumbled as I burst through the door, leaving mud everywhere. Then she started yelling.

'We found a dead bloke,' I said over the top of her and picked up the phone. Danny wasn't at the station so I called him at home and he said, 'What?' so I had to tell everything three times before he got off his fat arse and drove out. I told Mum, who had gone white and started crossing herself, to tell him to go up near Tim's Thicket because that's where it was and that's where we'd be waiting.

It had almost completely become night, but I rode back anyway. Dad and Eddy were sitting on an old, overgrown fallen log near it, trying to look away.

Nineteen nineteen

Rodney Small arrived in town for the first time on the back of his father's buggy, his hands gripping the dried out timber and rusted wire that they had loaded the evening before. Sweat soaked the old man's shirt as he snapped the leather of the reins, pulling up the horses. Rodney looked out from the buggy and stared at two council men in coats as they swept up the patterns of sand and dirt the rain had made on the bitumen. A policeman turned up and down the road telling off children. He had to clear the road for the march of returned soldiers and the restless crowd that met beneath the town hall clock. Rodney rubbed his eyes because everything had lost its shape, as though he was looking through the bottom of a bottle; it was unbelievable, different from the grey and green of the eucalypts, bigger than the bush dirt that stuck between his toes.

The old man shook the porter's hand and helped him unload the luggage. They climbed the flight of stairs that rose behind the public bar and found their room, a narrow cell at the end of a corridor filled with fading red carpet and the stench of old plaster. His father inspected the wardrobe and eyed the dampness that climbed the walls. He snorted at the bed, bending over it to push down on the springs. Rodney stood close to his father and ran his hands over the blanket, feeling that they were damp or maybe cold. The porter left with a coin, and they laid out their clothes on the bed. Rodney plastered his hair down with water, standing in front of the dirty, broken piece of mirror that rested on the bureau, before running after his father, who was descending into the pub.

The town was overflowing for the day; women in hats, old blokes in frayed suits, a triumphal arch set over the road for the soldiers to march through. Rodney's father stood near the bar and drank a jar of stout with two men he knew from a town to the north. Rodney gripped the cotton of his suit, watching as the sweat descended on them and they slapped each other's backs and laughed. The publican lined up the jars, laughing with them.

When the old man was drunk and his eyes had clouded over, Rodney Small slipped away past him, up the wooden stairs. The smell of beer turned his guts, and he covered his nose with his hand as he found a way out on to the roof to see the soldiers march below.

The brass band drove through the streets ahead of them; cymbals exploded, the crowd cheered, and children fled as if they were tied to one another. A cherry bomb cracked like a whip.

That night he lay next to his snoring Father, who had not noticed his son was gone. To Rodney, as he lay awake, it seemed that the world, or the way he saw it, had been altered. As he thought of the wood and wire in the buggy, cold against his face, he saw again the scrub that rushed past his skin; the approach of a tree, then the flickering image of it as it disappeared behind them. Rodney Small sensed that he was moving fast, faster than the horses had carried them. His father stirred and rolled onto his side and Rodney fell hard into sleep.

Nineteen forty two

American smoke filled the pub along with the crowing of old boilers who were slumping against sailors. You could smell the beer in the carpets and the furniture. As Rodney tried to leave, she blocked his exit. He had been uninterested as she arranged her hair while leaning her weight against the bar, but he lit her cigarette anyway and now she stood with her hands on her hips, tongue pushed into her cheek, trying a smile that the alcohol would not allow. Somehow her hair was tied back and falling out at the same time, her coat open to reveal part of her chest but holding it in by the loosely tied belt. He looked her up and down, but didn't try to push through her.

'Don't yer know what it means when you lend a girl a light?' She arched an eyebrow.

'I gave you a light, didn't I?'

'C'mon,' she said, reaching out to clutch his arm, pulling him into the cold air. 'I've got a flat in Essex Street.'

He walked close to her, working his arm around her waist, saying nothing but running his fingers over her back. She pressed herself into his side, gathering her arms up in front of her chest. Cold air blew into them from the side streets, filling the hems of their coats with animation. St Patrick's stood over them like an animal as they passed it, following the streets towards the ocean side of town. As they reached Essex Street, he kissed her neck, leaning down to her. She leant her head away, exposing the soft flesh for him.

'When do you leave?' she asked.

'Two Days.'

She examined him, thinking that in weeks he could be dead. While keeping her eyes fixed on him, she led him to a green door with a broken latch. The paint had faded and was falling loose. She slid her key in the lock and pulled him inside behind her. He gave her the impression that if she did not keep him moving, he would not overcome his own inertia. His eyes were round and lost, his hands heavy when she gripped them. She drew his head down to her, pressing her lips against his, hearing the door shut behind them.

'Are you scared?' she asked. Doors led off the hall. A hat stand with three felt hats. A mirror. She pulled him into a bedroom, the first room.

'Of You?'

She laughed. 'No. You know what. The War.'

He sensed that she wanted him to be. She would wrap him in her arms and pretend she could make him forget. 'That's a bit like asking a priest if he believes in God,' he said. 'You're never sure if he'll tell you the truth.' She kissed him, unbuttoned his coat. Her hand ran from his face down his chest.

'What I'm scared of,' he said, pausing to look hard at her, resting his eyes on the naked nape of her neck, 'is of after the war. Not the war itself.' He fingered the buttons and straps that held her in, felt the warm hardening of her muscles. She unfolded like a butterfly, her legs wrapping around his thighs. 'I'm not afraid of crossing the lines,' he continued. 'It's the ride home, packed in like cattle. What if I can't find a seat?'

She laughed, pressing him away. A car shuttled passed, unexpectedly filling the room with light. For a moment, everything was exposed like a photograph: the war brown walls, the carefully stacked pile of dirty dishes and the unarranged, broken furniture. He undid her as the light faded, not as suddenly as it had appeared. He untied her, lifted away her clothes as though a breeze had breathed them into life, filling them like sheets on a line.

'My fear,' she breathed into his ear, 'is that the war will never end, it will just go on and on.' She pulled him tightly to her chest. 'Here I was just thinking that I'd do you a good turn and look what you've got me saying.' She rolled him off and searched beside the bed for cigarettes. Another car passed, bouncing light off the walls, re-exposing the room. He glimpsed the stretch of her thighs in a half-light compound of shadow and brightness that gave them the impression of transparency. He thought that if he reached out his hand it would pass right through and push into the blue pillows beneath her. She was an image, a mirage, he thought, as he waited for the car to pass and for the light to die.

Nineteen nineteen

Down in the laneway, the grocer's daughter felt the grime of the wall as he pressed her back against it with the stabbing of his hips. She feared for her white linen dress, now stretched tightly across her back and gathered around her waist. Watching the parade passing from the corner of her eye, she tried to focus on the coloured uniforms of the soldiers and not the greys and browns of the crowd.

'Bernie,' she hissed into is ear, 'take it slowly, or you'll ruin me best dress.' He grunted, turning his face away from her. She gripped him even more tightly, but only so she didn't slide down the wall.

'Keep still, for Christ's sake,' said Bernie, readjusting the girth of his stance, re-hoisting her onto him, driving her harder into the wall. 'Stop yer wrigglin'.'

Gripping her thighs, and with his eyelids pressed tightly shut, he was careful to notice how she curved and how she felt in his hands. Rubbing his head into her neck, he whispered at her, 'Mary...Oh God, Jesus...' Three children ran down the alley, shouting at each other, too young and too excited to notice. As she felt him quivering to a halt, she arched her back to receive him, groaning into his neck if only from the pain of it and the tears she felt rip open in her dress.

Peering down at them, Rodney Small locked his hands around the gutter with his white knuckles. He watched her dress drawn tightly against the top of her thighs and her bare shins and shoes clasped tightly behind his arse. Her arms constantly rearranged themselves, gripping at his neck. As the man had quickened his pace against the woman, Rodney ground himself against the asbestos beneath him. He imitated the man, pretending he was thrusting into her. Growing hard against the resistance of the roof, a foreign pleasure overwhelmed him, as if two giant hands had wrung him out, squeezed him down. As they stopped writhing against the wall, Rodney felt his knees and elbows inflame with a pain he did not expect. The man crushed himself into her, his arse jerking with the struggle.

'Mary...Oh God, Mary...' gasped the man.

'Shhh,' she hissed. 'Stop yer pantin'.' She looked back up the alley; a few women trickled past on the main street, pulling children along by their hands. A father yelled. Rodney shifted his hands on the gutter, preparing to slip away. Mary caught the motion, glanced upwards and saw the top of his head peering down at her with two round eyes and eight white knuckles gripping the rusty gutter. As he met her eyes she smiled, feeling the sweat collect on the back of her neck. Then he disappeared. She heard the crack of breaking asbestos as he ran across the roof. She pulled Bernie's head into her so he could not hear him fleeing, or notice her laughter.

Clamouring down a drainpipe, he tore his pants and scratched his leg open. He ran down the street away from the hotel, pulling out his shirt to cover himself, smoothing himself down and fixing his nest of hair. He thought she would have been angry, looking up to find him staring at her. Why did she smile? She must have thought me pathetic. He imagined himself driving her against the wall, showing her. Maybe that is why she smiled? Perhaps she wanted the twist of limbs that he pressed out in his imagination, compelling her against the crumbling bricks.

Later, as it grew dark, he wandered down to look for her, but found no one. He thought of her thighs wrapped around the unkempt body of the man and how her dress had gathered, edging higher as she moved. He imagined her lips parting to smile at him. He thought that they could have been statues, but in motion, moving so slowly, almost as if you could not see them move unless you looked away, then looked back again.

Nineteen forty two

Small screwed up his face to grapple with the landscape roughing past the dirty windows of the train. Without a sudden stretch of open land, or a gap in the foliage that revealed the middle distance, it all flitted by like disjointed images, like a pack of cards thrown up into the air. Trees, bushes, hedges, peasants became abruptly perceptible, then disappeared.

Asleep beside Small, a soldier snored, his breath rearranging the carelessly sculptured hairs of his moustache. A bible lay open in his lap and his hand rested lifelessly between its pages. Adjacent him, two others played cards. They dealt hands with increasing velocity in a contest that was more to do with speed than chance.

'Got ya there, matey,' said the black haired soldier, revealing his hand and stretching his back. The other huffed. 'Look at him, eh,' indicating Small with a dry, ruddy thumb. 'Not said a single word since we left. Not even a bloody 'ullo.' He leant in closer to Small, still cradling his winning hand. 'You right there, matey? Got the jitters, eh?'

'Leave him alone, poor bastard,' said the other, shuffling his cards out of order. 'He'll be shitting in his pants soon enough, I reckon. You were a bloody poor bastard like that once as well.' Darkness and the rattle of a tunnel disturbed the sleeping soldier. He shifted his weight, his mouth slapping opened and closed, his hands hitching the belt of his trousers and knocking the bible to the floor.

'Yeah. He's just got a touch of the nerves. You'll be right, mate. Happened to us all. He's a bit stunned, that's all.'

Small swallowed an upward ebb of bile. He tried not to look at the soldiers, but felt the need to say something. Real men feel their fear in their heads, his father had said, not in their hearts. *My fear explodes in the earth, floats down like a rain of dirt. I feel it in my bowel like I could shit it out.* He thought of his father reclining like a cat in his great padded leather chair. He thought of him sniffing the atmosphere for the last damp trace of pipe smoke and opening the book that he cradled in his lap. He thought of him closing his eyes, forgetting the print on the pages, instead conjuring the ceaseless thunder of war and the trains barrelling through its midst.

Fear had gripped him the day he left.

Ignoring his Mother, he had smoked a cigarette, smoothing out his khakis with a quick, nervous hand. His kit lay at his feet on the gravel. 'This war business will be over by Christmas,' he said after dragging a mouthful of smoke deeply into his lungs. 'So please stop crying, mother.' He draped an arm around her neck, letting it rest on her shoulders, flicking ash off his cigarette. She pushed her face into his armpit, sobbing and gulping down air. His father stamped his feet to get warm; one, then the other, drumming them on the ground. They stood huddled together at the gate, expiring hot breath into the cold morning air. From beyond the gate they heard the splutter of the car and the spray of dirt carved up by tyres.

She sobbed into his uniform.

'Let him go,' said his father, raising his voice. He blew warm air in into his cupped hands. 'Be quiet, woman, and leave the boy alone. Hurry, son, you can't miss the boat.' Somehow, his father understood, shaking his hand, looking at him for what could have been the last time.

'Don't worry, Mum. I'll see you soon enough.'

The car drew up next to them and Small climbed in. His Father grunted as he hoisted the heavy kit onto his son's lap. 'Remember…' he begun to say but stopped, placing a hand on his shoulder, gripping it gently. Small nodded. As the car drove away, he glanced over his shoulder and saw, for the briefest moment, his mother held in his father's arms, his head bent into her hair.

In the train, the soldiers dealt another hand and Small sat paralysed, his eyes fixed to the images stirring on the other side of the window.

'Don't worry, son,' said the black haired soldier. 'You'll know all about it soon enough.'

Nineteen forty eight

Dirty curtains billowed in the open windows, and outside the weathercock ground around its axis. He sat naked, examining the fleshy stump where his right arm once was, examining the yellow stretch of his three other limbs. Yawning, he stood, putting his other hand through his hair, feeling for length. The yard cock crowed, his dog barked.

'Bloody hell,' he thought, because morning dawned on him, throwing light onto his face, filling the room with a brightness dulled by filthy glass. 'Fuckin' already.' He threw the blanket over the bed, covering the mattress, but not straightening its edges. He slammed the window shut and waited for the curtain to fall still, then ran his hand over his chest, pulling at the hairs, eyeing them in the shaving mirror that rested on the table against the books.

Then he opened the cupboard, found the leather case, and pulled his rifle from it. Without thinking he walked out the door, leaving it open behind him, heading for the bush. He drove himself through the lupins, crushing them beneath the naked soles of his feet, feeling the bite as they stuck him. Out in the middle of a field he paused, looked down at his body and laughed. 'Why do I do these things?' he asked aloud, but in a way that suggested the answer was always the same and that for the first time he knew what it was.

His mind filled with images, each occurring quickly, one after the other. He saw a couple against a wall, the sun setting over the murk of London, his father unloading coils of wire and swearing at the horses. He turned and headed off into the bush, up the track to where it curled around the scarp. He closed his eyes as he walked, feeling each step after the other, disappearing into the green and the grey.

Nineteen forty four

Of all the things that could have occurred to him as the shell exploded, he was surprised that it was a picture of his old man, an impression that formed itself from nothing and rose steadily within him. His Father was ceaselessly arranging his hands, folding them and refolding them, his entire weight shifting in his chair.

He said, 'Boy, there are some things you won't learn for many years.' The study had walls made of different types of stone, some grey, some brown, of different sizes, slotted together randomly between carelessly trowelled cement. Yellow candlelight illuminated the vast wooden desk and the untidy piles of paper that covered it.

'Some things you will never learn.' Rodney kept his eyes fixed to the floor, his hands clasped tensely to his front, pressing against the flannel of his pyjama pants. 'Are you listening to me, boy?'

'Yes,' said Rodney, not raising his eyes to him.

'Some things you will learn from books, some things you will learn from me, and some things you will learn from others.' Rodney nodded. My Old Man has grown so fat, he thought. His gut spilled out of his chair and his face flushed with blood when he had to re-arrange his girth. 'Some things you will learn and then just as quickly forget. This even happens to me.' My Old Man, he thought. Like the side of a house. He dared look up through his eyebrows. 'But, my boy, if you learn anything that will help you in life it is this: pay attention. You must open your ears and listen, do you hear?'

'Yes, Dad,' he said quietly, recasting his eyes on the floor, sensing it would soon be over, 'I'll pay attention.'

'Good. Then you'll learn other things if you pay attention. Then everyone will consider you a clever, smart young fella.' He curled his sweating palms around the arms of his chair and again repositioned the uncomfortable burden of his arse. 'So, my boy, you will listen.'

'Yes.'

He imagined his father as a building, whitewashed, with thatches. He pictured him as a mud hut; quivering in a storm with all its weight, ready to slide into itself.

'Good boy,' whispered his father, smiling at last. He stretched apart his heavy arms and Rodney fell between them, hugging his broad, soft chest. 'You are my little boy, aren't you? Barely higher than my waist and already so smart.'

He's not like a house, he thought, sinking into his weight, rubbing his face against his bristly cheek; he is like a stack of hay. He is a bonfire waiting to be lit. The old man released his grip and Rodney ran down the corridors away from him, towards his bedroom, his fists clenched tightly as he scurried.

He slammed the door behind him, climbed onto the bed and tested the latch on the wooden window frame. Finding the window unlocked, he swung it open, but slowly to prevent the creaking of its rusted through hinges. A gust of cold air pierced the room and blew through him. Burrowing into his bed, he let the cold numb his face before his Mother, hearing the wind banging his door, came in and closed the window, kissing his forehead. He drifted to sleep.

In the murk beyond the line, Small pushed himself into the mud, seeking the wet coolness to soothe the ferocious burning of his wound. Shells exploded in brown clouds of dirt with tails of dirty smoke and, for seconds afterwards, sand, rock and flesh rained down. Feet splashed around him as they ran past. The muffled shouting of charging or wounded men filled the gaps between sudden explosions. His ears buzzed and rang, damaged by the noise.

'Move yer fucken' arse, Tommy,' yelled a man, falling into Small's ditch, before seeing the writhing bloodied mass of his arm and shoulder. 'Jesus

Christ, boy,' he said, but he could not be heard above the howling. 'You'll be alright, boyo...Medic...we'll get yer back across...I think he's still conscious...Can you hear, me boyo?' Small groaned as a shell exploded nearby. Two other soldiers gripped him by the ankles and pulled him towards the lines.

His absence hung humidly in the air. Mrs Small, his Mother, turned the tumbler in her hands, regarding its nature, put it to her lips and let the whiskey warm her. She could feel his absence on her skin. It became suffused with the whiskey and, when she woke numbly each morning, it laced her breath. When she closed her eyes, she saw his surly bulk; thick arms, strong back and fattened waist.

Small could not see through the mud in his eyes, but felt the burning of his arm and shoulder. 'Hoist him onta the fuckin' stretcher.' He thought of his Mother. He remembered the image of his Father sitting at his desk. Soldiers yelled and clattered around him and he felt as though he was tumbling.

From within the newly fallen darkness of her room, her hand stretches out towards him. His eyes still rest where her thighs would be, but now he can see nothing, only feel the warmth of her pressing fingers. Somehow, she wraps around him and he presses her against an invisible wall. 'Here I was just thinking that I would do you a good turn,' she says, breathing into his ear, 'and look what you've got me saying.' Her lips are wet, she is moving against him. He waits for a turning car to throw light on her through the window, but instead he comes trembling to a stand still, his hands resting on her thighs, just beneath the dress gathering above her waist. His hands search for it, seeking the soft harshness of cotton, but it is impossible in the darkness. 'Look what you've got me saying.' She releases him into the emptiness. He thinks if he thrusts out his hand it would pass right through her, into the blue pillows.

The Osk Whale

I marvel at the precision of my actions, my seemingly unconscious ability to select a particular and direct outcome and then enact it, like opening a closed door or getting dressed in the morning. I think of all the incidental and yet very possible interruptions that could take place within such machinations but invariably never seem to do so. I know I should not marvel at such things. I am a grown man of thirty-six years old who should be far beyond such simple musings. It is just that in these unbalancing moments of wonder where all motion and time around me slow considerably I am almost struck dumb by sensing again what connections of impulse and instinct in my psychological body allow me to move through my physical days with such outwardly apparent precision.

For some reason this disabling amazement at such simple things feels very close to me today. The midday air in the office is cold and brisk and the exposed skin on my hands and face is tightened by the chill. The green waterproof material of my jacket swishes against itself as I move through the brick corridor towards the front door. I reach for the handle to the outside world and grab it exactly, not a millimetre off in any direction. The door handle is cold and clean and bare, a round smooth object occupying its own definitive area in space.

A report has come through to the ranger's office that an Osk Whale is trapped in Baker's Hole. This is such a fantastical, unlikely event that I am convinced it is a hoax. Millions of years ago the imposing and relentless waterways now named Bass Strait discovered a particular weak spot in the sandstone cliffs bordering southwest Victoria. The freezing waters of this particularly notorious stretch of ocean continuously threw its might against these sandstone walls and in doing so gradually ate away at the rock, eventually creating a tunnel through the land approximately forty meters long. At this point the remaining land above the end of this tunnel was also significantly weak enough to collapse, leaving a large exposed crater open to the world, now known as Baker's Hole. The sea continues to enter the hole via the tunnel, ending in spectacular tidal clashes with the walls of this natural amphitheatre, before returning back towards Bass Strait with a fury, thumping into the next rush of water entering the underground passage. It is now one of many popular tourist attractions on a breathtaking piece of coastline and part of the Port Campbell National Park, where I am head ranger.

In my current state of distraction I am reluctant to give this report any credit, although it is a very imaginative piece of story telling. There has not been a sighting of an Osk Whale near Australia for fifteen years and not in the world for five. The last proven sighting was video footage of a Japanese fishing trawler pulling up two of the creatures on to it's deck and the common international opinion is that the species is now extinct, the prize of an Osk Whale being a far too valuable a trophy for the whale hunting nations to resist. There are many remarkable things about the Osk Whale – its massive annual migratory path, their lifetime partnerships, its intricate internal make-up that allows the mammal to stay submerged the longest of all its cousins but, as is the case with many extinct species, it was primarily hunted for its appearance. Its skin is covered with varying sizes of black, brown and white spots, not unlike the underbelly of a leopard seal, though the whale's body is more iridescent than its smaller cousins. But spectacularly, the whale's most noticeable and instantly recognisable feature is the two horns it has protruding from its snout, one above the other. It is similar in this way to the Narwhale although the Narwhale only has the one horn and does not utilize it in spectacular displays of masculine jousting strength just about the surface of the water as the Osk whale does. These remarkable battles were the stuff of documentary makers' wet dreams, magnificent proof of nature's power and beauty, thrashing heads and striking sparks. These horns were in fact over developed teeth and, when it was alive, caused it to be one of the most romanticised and referred to animals on the planet. There are countless myths connected to the Osk Whale – a sighting will give a lifetime of good luck, wearing a piece of its horn around your neck will make you immortal, eating it's flesh will assure you of giving birth to twins, but of course no myth is as strong as having the prestige of mounting a set of Osk Whale horns above your fireplace. The unfortunate, rapid demise of the Osk Whale was inevitable and seemingly in no time at all they had disappeared off the face of the planet.

So I have no expectation about the validity of this current report. I have certainly never heard of anything similar happening on this coastline and I have lived here all my life. Possibly some half-blind tourist has seen a large disorientated fur seal thrashing about at the entrance to Baker's Hole, although I guess that in itself would be a rarity… anyway nothing will come of it and I expect this trip will just turn into a routine check of the park.

At this time of year the cold sweeps in from the deep south and taints any obstacle in its path. Everything in the ute is cold to touch, the door the steering wheel the vinyl seats through my grey trousers. As I pull on to the main road that will take me towards the site I have to wait to allow two cars to pass in the same direction as I wish to go. I know both cars and the two people driving them. One is a local farmer, the other a local shop owner. I suspect the ranger's station is not the first place to hear the rumour of the Osk Whale. I have never been a fan of large crowds and I hope that word has not spread quickly enough to cause a gathering of excited and disappointed onlookers.

My concerns however are not appeased on the way down. I am passed by another two cars and have two behind me when I finally turn left on to the kilometre long gravel road that takes you to the Hole (it is approximately twenty six kilometres from the ranger's office to here). Again the two cars that passed me were local although the two behind me are not. All suspicions are answered when I pull into Baker's car park and see every available parking space and then some occupied – word has clearly spread and in a small coastal community like this, the desire not to be left out is strong. There are so many vehicles that some latecomers have simply driven off the road and parked right across the natural vegetation. I decide to let it go for the moment given the possible situation, but it is one of the things that annoys me excessively as a park ranger. I leave the ute further up the carpark feeling increasingly uncomfortable about this blatant disregard of the park's rules and by the truly surprising number of people present.

I am not one to blow my own trumpet but I do have a wide knowledge of the parks vegetation and fauna and often find myself in conversations of length with visitors on such matters, but the vast number of people around today knocks me off balance and I don't know where to start or who to approach. As I am walking down the path towards the gathering clutch of unfamiliar people a youngish man in chequered pants and sports jacket turns to me and says, 'Crazy stuff hey man?' Such opened ended introductory remarks like these always stump me and as much as I wish I could think of a casual reply I cannot and end up simply smiling awkwardly toward him. He seems disappointed with my effort and I must remember that in a situation like this I am regarded as a figure of authority, that I am expected to have answers and have the ability to make decisions. The distant roar of the ocean mingles with the crunching of gravel underfoot and I watch my steps closely, careful that I should not be seen to stumble.

The open circular top of Baker's Hole has a diameter of approximately forty metres (I know this because I am required to measure it every four months to keep track of the rate of erosion). There are onlookers all around the circumference of the opening, all peering down into its centre. The viewing platforms at either end are full of people and on the sides in some places they are five or six deep. Some are foolishly sitting on the other side of the waist high protective fence, a metre or two away from the steep drop in to the freezing water. A few of those in this position move back on to the other side of the barrier when they see me approach but only those closest to me – the people who are further away have no such concerns and remain transfixed at the spectacle below. There are many locals present but also a surprising number of tourists and out-of-towners as well. I cannot imagine they have taken the four and half hour drive from the city just for this, I cannot imagine how rumour would have spread that fast, and yet it is hard to believe it is just coincidence as well. Whatever the reason Baker's Hole has never seen so many people at the one time before. There is the hum and rise and fall of a murmuring crowd in the air with the occasional shriek of an excited or annoyed child bracketing the noise.

As I approach even closer the crowd parts and I am let through easily to the safety fence. I feel my presence become more widely known and there is a noticeable shift in the energy of the crowd, some momentary easing of tension. I climb the fence to get a clearer look and there, there it is, there can be no denying it – there is a fully grown Osk Whale caught in the heaving ocean waters of Baker's Hole. Stunned, I feel a cold blast of biting wind on my face and the noise of the crowd disperses around me. Incredible.

…but after the first few moments of sheer amazement at such a bizarre and unlikely spectacle what becomes readily apparent is that the poor animal is in great distress. Under panic or alarm the Osk Whale will turn a full circle at the surface of the water and having only watched for a minute or so I have already seen the sheer white underbelly of the whale roll twice round toward me. The confined area of Baker's Hole is clearly disturbing the mature animal (the whale is around seven metres long) and the constant and severe rise and fall of the swell seems to be disorientating it – however the whale stumbled in here is clearly as much of a mystery to itself as it is to its public. The noise of the crowd (which I originally heard as calls and remarks of appreciation and wonder) returns to me amplified and now has curt edges to its hum and there are many shocks of breath taken in as the whale thrashes its body around in the thumping waters below. When the animal bucks its head and in fact strikes one side wall with its upper horn an anxious groan echoes throughout the crowd.

I am on my haunches near the edge of the hole. The whale is truly magnificent but I am also very aware of the rising discomfort that surrounds me. When the whale again makes a full body roll near the surface of the water a number of red marks can clearly be seen dotted along its flanks. The breath coming from the whale's blowhole is constant and frantic, the tail thrashes and the two rare horns on its distressed head nod and shake in the air, perhaps attempting to engage an invisible foe. Its panic is understandable but I doubt anyone watching had even considered that this would be the case before they arrived. I imagine they envisaged a gentle scene with a rare animal displaying its serene majesty for our pleasure, not this upsetting situation of a terrified animal in distress.

Without realising it my appearance has in fact caused some real commotion in the crowd. A middle aged woman with thick brown frizzled hair and wide tracksuit pants has pushed her way through the crowd and then, when she is close enough, bails me up over the fence (I had never been in a situation in my life where the term 'bails me up' was more appropriate). She wants to know what the hell was going on and what the hell I was going to do about it the animal could not be left in this predicament it was upsetting all the children watching not to mention it was upsetting itself and furthermore what took you so long to get here if you got here earlier you may have been able to rectify the situation sooner and spare all this unnecessary concern but now at least that you are here you bloody well better do something about and quickly do you hear me?... She is seemingly quite upset about the situation herself. She lets forth with such a tirade that if the people within earshot were not thinking as she was when she started her verbal spray, they certainly will be by the time she finishes. I feel that all of this is a little unfair and I am about to point out to her that I personally have not in fact had anything to do with the whale getting trapped in the pool when a sickening crack emanates up and outwards from the direction of the water. As one, the crowd shrieks. I turn my attention away from the woman back to the whale. It is writhing and thrashing about in the water almost uncontrollably and only in glimpses do I realise its bottom horn has snapped off, broken on impact against a sandstone wall. The horn disappears, sinking underneath the constant white hands of the ocean.

Young children turn their faces into the legs of their parents. The brown haired woman escalates her tirade and more and more people began to take notice. Down below the broken Osk Whale shakes its wide rare head from side to side. An old bearded man yells out at me across the water, demanding to know what I'm going to do. A few families begin to leave the scene, to return to their cars and leave this unexpected sadness. Against the biting wind people hold tissues to their faces while young vicious boys peer over the edge for a better view.

I myself do not know what is going to happen, or if in fact there is anything to do at all. The whale obviously cannot find its own way out again and I can't see a clear safe way to direct it. I briefly consider air lifting it to safety but it is far too dangerous to place any divers in the hole given the animal's distress and the aggressive force of the ocean. What else could happen apart from the whale scaring itself to exhaustion then eventual death? I wonder how many other people watching this tragedy have the same thought and as I look around at the shouting heaving crowd everything around and inside me slows down. All the voices and all the surrounding noise joins together into one far distant muffled hum. I feel the coarseness of my trousers with the cold palms of my hands, on either side of my skin. I wonder if it is always this messy and unplanned when great events unfold. In clear, precise slow motion I watch the terrified animal ram a part of the sheer stone wall surrounding it and snap its last remaining horn from its head. Hands go up to disgusted faces, people bend and bow to check that it is not their backs that have broken. I stand, drowning with noise and emotion. I feel the tugs at my clothes and the screams in my ears as I walk slowly back to the ute to call for help.

I have spoken to all relevant authorities and I have been told what to do. I have verification and approval from every necessary party – government offices have spoken with conservation groups and so on, everything was decided and agreed to. I have to wait twenty minutes for police protection but once they arrive there is no longer any need to hesitate or wait – orders must be carried out.

It has been decided that the situation is hopeless. Tragic yes, but hopeless. Nothing can realistically be done to save the whale. As I have been told and reassured, yes it was a sad event but strange things happen such is life etc all common sense logical comments from people half a country away. However there is no need for the situation to be prolonged either. The animal is clearly in a distressed and helpless state and its plight is unduly affecting all those who have come to see this rare and magnificent beast. Therefore the decision has been made that in the best interests of the animal and the community the whale should be destroyed, and quickly. As I am without doubt the nearest and most suitable candidate for the job, it has also been decided that I should be the one to complete the task. That is, the task of eradicating very possibly the last example of a unique and timeless natural species.

The crowd is still wild and erratic when I return to the hole, some crying some cheering all excited and braying. As I return, I watch my feet place themselves perfectly on the ground, one foot in front of the other. My fingers tense and release on command on the cold smooth metal of the rifle. Two policemen walk along either side of me, highlighting rather than protecting me. I look around and see no familiar faces anymore, just eyes spit teeth and hair. I approach the edge of Baker's and kneel down perfectly.

I am allowed as many shots as it takes. I place the box of very large bullets beside my left knee. The whale itself seems more subdued now, maybe resigned already to its undeniable fate. The hum of noise that surrounds comes to me as if from underwater. I raise the rifle to my shoulder and aim.

Aware of the precisions of my actions like never before, I prepare to fire and take my dubious place in history.

A Short History of Black

1.

Dobie comes out front, a blackened ghoul in shining grease and trainsmoke. I try to tell him, all of it and none of it, that there was a man who went beneath the train, that I caught deep in my guts the sound of him hitting, but my mouth won't move except to grapple with the air. My arms and legs are still, the engine has come to rest, but not the head of steam rising in its belly. I look at Dobie but I don't know what it is I'm seeing and my mouth keeps moving.

'He tried to move out the way,' I say at last. There was a street lamp not far that showed him up on the rails but only after I could have stopped. It showed him up hearing the clock and drone through his skin, then our train light moved on him and I saw his old drunk face, suddenly sober as he tried to move out the way. What have I become here, so close to the last stop, a killer of old men? Dobie has it written on his face, could he have heard his cries? We took him fast, I know he's dead, we could never have pulled up short, I could never have stopped. My mouth opens again and I feel the cries I could not hear like fists thrown in my chest.

Old drunk dead on the rails.

He must have been half asleep, feeling the steel of our train before he saw it properly, unable to leap aside as it bore down on him. From where I sit I feel part of the engine, part of what hit him. He tried to run, but could barely move, drunken bastard. Dobie scowls. He puts the charcoal stumps of his fingers into his oily hair and says, 'I'll never get home, you bastard, you should've stopped.'

The ground is far away as I climb down the ladder towards it. I can see myself in the light of the same street lamp as Dobie comes down behind me. We look around and see him tossed clear, not breathing, his legs bent in a way they could not have gone if he had been alive.

Blood is over his face and through his beard as if it had been thrown from a bucket. I know he is dead. His still eyes are open and unblinking, as an animal's would be. The clean smell of alcohol comes off him and sits like a fist at the back of my throat. He is like every other drunk, the dozens

I've seen anchored to platforms, or stumbling up wooden steps to the station. His beard is long and his coat is old and full of pockets. His shoulders would have been stooped; you can tell this even in the way he has come to rest.

'You wait here,' says Dobie. 'I'll try to find a copper.' And he recedes into the murk, leaving me the heavy sound of his boots.

I sit with the old man, staring into his red eyes that will not close. I cannot guess how long Dobie has been gone, but I hear a delivery truck somewhere and the night changes from its utter depth to something stained with brown, like the man's coat. I touch his hand to say I touched a dead man in the dark, even if I will say it only to myself. Something of his stillness comes over me also, a motionlessness that I find in the stones around us and now in the engine that has come to rest. We are all alike, I think: the drunk, the train, the air that is not moved by a wind, and the train driver chilling the seat of his pants in the early morning beside the breathless fool he has murdered with his sober drowsiness. I remember to wipe my hand that had touched his hand on my trousers, fearing that by touching him I had made myself guilty. But what could come from him to me?

Closing my eyes for a moment, I see nothing, just the moving blackness behind the lids. I almost reach out for the moving shapes. Seeing nothing is a way of not thinking. Seeing black is not seeing the death I've done, the bloodspill in the man's beard. A prayer almost rises to my lips, I swear, but I swallow it whole. I cannot hear prayers except through the seat of my pants.

I look through his pockets, searching for something bearing his name. Broken glass from a smashed bottle cuts my finger. Inside his coat, near to where his heart was, I find a copy of the Bible, bound in dirty leather. What trick is this? What is it that I have done? Could this man have turned a corner, away from the bottle, when I ran him down, knocking the life from him? Dobie wouldn't care, except that we will be late home, but he didn't kill a man, his fingers weren't on the reins.

I hear his heavy boots returning on the gravel.

'I've sent for the coppers,' says Dobie when he is near enough. 'I can't believe we're late because of this drunken bastard. Why should we even stop? Someone else's bloody problem, eh.'

The Bible is small and I fit it into my pocket before Dobie can see it. I've killed a man on his first steps at life. If they could've shaved him and found him a suit, but he lies here dead, no words of God returning to his lips, and I think of Lazarus sitting upright in his hole, terrified that not all of him had returned alive, but in the keenness of his animation he had left something of himself dead, a sense of himself on the other side. But the old drunk has left part of himself living within me, near the breast of a stranger.

Suddenly, there is a suffocating weight in the absence of light, a ton of dark that falls onto me from a height. The absence that drives the dead man, the lack of animation, drives me also. We are defined by stillness, a vacuum, the funeral weight of black.

Dobie comes next to me and shakes me by the arm. He is speaking. I look to him and see the letters he makes of his lips. He is a kind of blackness I can see because of the churlish brown morning light. I look again at the old man, who is so much of me, and think of his life as it ended, as I watched it moments ago, scrabbling in the firm lights of the train's coming.

2.

'Edward Withers,' says Ruth, breathing it over her teeth, her anger like a dog off its leash. Exhaustion has begun to put its hands on me, as Ruth also reaches up and grabs me by the collar. I am as still as I can make myself.

'Don't touch me,' I say, feeling the rising blood redden my face. 'I've killed a man and don't need a woman to give me more grief than I'm worth.' The lids of her eyes become narrow. 'Fetch me something to eat. I'll be in me chair.' I fall into the old pile of wood and leather at which I had pointed.

Ruth, who's not much to look at, her pale skin and fingers raw from scrubbing and soap and such. The only mention I'd make of Ruth is the animal black of her eyes. My house is a corridor with three rooms off to the side and whenever I think of her standing in it, I think of her waiting behind the door, anger clouding her face with its red flush. She knows better than to keep at me, so she goes to the stove and cuts me the bread she has been browning, and brings it on a plate. Then she stands in the doorway, shifting her weight from one foot to the other, working her hands together as if she is kneading dough.

'I don't believe you've killed a man,' she says at last, consumed by a slow energy. 'I'd say you've not the mind to go through with it, Edward Withers.'

'I ran him down with the engine. I wouldn't expect you to believe me, Ruth. You're a curse. Bring me the bottle of beer I never finished last night.'

She comes over to me and puts her warm hand on my shoulder, and I think, everything has a dead weight about it, even her when she comes to rest. I think of how I first saw her, bundled in her coat, gloves and hat, waiting for the train in the five o'clock crowd.

'I've already finished that bottle meself,' she says and takes her hand away. I see it leaping from me.

I put the bread in my mouth, thinking about every piece, watching her pull her woollen shawl tighter around her shoulders. Then she leaves the room and brings a fresh bottle of beer, pulling the cork so I can put it straight to my lips and watch her as I drink.

The fireplace is nothing but embers and she stands near it, drawing up what's left of the heat. She's like a burning coal, letting off dull warmth, moving from one place to another as the charcoal around her collapses, one instant glowing red, another black and cold.

'It makes me sick waiting for you to get home.' She folds and unfolds her arms. 'Yer trains run on time, but what about you? In and out when you please.' The candle light is yellow on the walls, though brighter when she puts a match to the oil lamp. 'And I'm here sitting in the dark, the child in bed, wondering when you're going to appear, counting every bloody minute.'

'Didn't you hear me?' I shout, leaping up out of the chair. When her eyes fall away from me and she is quiet except for her quick breath, I fall back into it, becoming part of it, a piece of the wood and leather also. I take the Bible from my pocket and hold it where she can get a good look. 'This was in his coat when I killed him. I saw him as he tried to get out the way. He's not just a drunk now. It's like he'd seen Jesus Christ himself and not the engine bearing down on him.'

She takes the Bible out of my hand and rifles through it. 'You should've stopped. You'll regret killing a man with a Bible in his coat.'

I summon myself up from the chair, an apparition, and go to the laundry. I fill the basin with cold water and begin to shave. The rusty blade passes over my skin, over the soap that won't lather. The child begins to cry and I hear Ruth murmuring, comforting with the thick oil of her voice. I shake the blade in water and wash off hair, then return it to my face. I can see in the small mirror hanging by a length of string. Ruth comes up behind me and touches my shirtless back. Soap is up my arms. I wash my face and neck, then powder myself dry. I put on my cleanest shirt and sit down in the chair once more.

Nothing but to look at her, carrying the child on her hip, looking at me now and then as though I am a stranger in my own house. What has changed in me that she has to stare with her black eyes that look as if they might leave her body and pass right through me?

I stand and straighten myself. In the laundry I oil my hair and comb it. Ruth hovers around, staring but not coming into the room, I see what must be her hair from the corner of my eye, so I go out the back door and let the screen close behind me. I jump the back fence, the dirt getting on my clean hands, the sun getting warm.

My name comes out of her mouth, an animal at my heels. I've remembered to take the book from where she'd put it down and stuff it in the pocket of my trousers. I see now where all of this will end, all of it and none of it.

3.

The copper looks down his moustache at the dead man and prods him with his boot. He huffs at Dobie who is beginning to look nervous.

'Who's the driver?' asks the copper. Dobie points at me and the copper turns, not his head, but his entire body. 'You've killed him.' He walks over and stops so close I can smell him. His bloodshot eyes bulge for a moment and his lips harden. 'You must've seen him. Or were you asleep?'

Dust has settled on the old drunk's body, the grey of it mixed in with drying blood. I saw him. I saw the last moment like a spray of water that was in the air for an instant, and then settled on the ground.

'I saw him too late. I couldn't stop. I tried.'

The copper holds his breath.

Two men from the railway are walking up the line, quickening their pace when they see the copper's uniform. Everything is converging on me, or that's how it seems. Dobie moves nervously, as though he is about to bolt.

'As long as you weren't asleep,' the copper says. He turns to watch the men coming closer.

'He's our best man,' says Dobie. 'He couldn't sleep on the job, even if he wanted.'

I sit on the ground, releasing my weight, letting the stones puncture me. I cover my eyes and block out the early light. Dobie is muttering, we'll never get home, we'll never get home.

The two men are closer. There is a tall man with a grey suit and a filthy signalman without a hat. The first is Mr Spurling and the other must be the new man from Midland, come to see a drunk killed, which seems to a signalman the only interesting thing that could ever happen. The signalman says nothing, but rubs his stubble and stares at the dead man, as though he is thinking, there I go but for the grace of God.

'What a bloody tragedy,' says Spurling, while looking down beyond the engine to see what load we had been pulling. 'A man is dead and we are bloody hours behind. You'll be held responsible, Withers. This is too much. Too much.' The signalman keeps fingering at his stubble.

The copper and Spurling walk out of earshot and they talk with flourishes of their hands and frowns that pinch their faces into knots. At one point, they are both looking at me and the copper is speaking and Spurling is nodding his head, his jowls reddening as they quiver. I see them set against the brick walls that are stacked away from the railway lines and the plumes of dark smoke that billow from the factories. Even the tree I can see beside the far road becomes like a finger that is accusing me.

'Don't worry, mate,' says Dobie, seeing it all come over me. I look at him and see he is perspiring. He hates standing still. All he wants is to get home, or at least to move away from the sprawl of the dead man.

The copper comes over and takes his pencil and notebook from a pocket. I tell him my name and address and everything I saw, right down to the slow terror in his eyes and the way his body leapt too late. Spurling stands nearby and listens, glancing at his watch, thinking of the load that is going nowhere. For him nothing ever runs on time, everything moves according to its own schedule. Even me, even the drunk who is now helpless and lying dead, a useless, seamless, empty sack of nothing. I won't be hurried. Spurling's watch is a law for him and nothing to me. The copper writes everything down and then with a wave of his hand, seems to say we can go.

Dobie looks at his feet and hurries. I take one last look at the drunk and then I am also gone.

4.

I leap over the back fence and turn to watch my name escape from her mouth. Then I run, imagining her voice leaving footprints in the soil alongside my own. My breath is drawn hard over my teeth. I follow the lane as it comes out onto the street and turn down towards the river, heading for the empty Lacey House, thinking of the silence handled by the old walls and the pale, dry roof. They moved east months ago. The times I drank with the old man up in his room. He'd pour out a measure into a tumbler and watch as I worked it in my hands, drinking it at last, feeling the ball of warmth work through my guts. I walk through the front gate, into the yard still kept by someone, thinking of the old man and his decanter.

Ruth is like the grey eucalypt that emerges in the yard, overlooking everything, too loud with her silence. I try to escape it by forcing the front door off its rusty hinges and pulling it closed behind me as best I can. The leaves on its grey fingers are still there outside the door and they unsettle me in the same way that Lacey said he never liked the awful presence of the tree. Too close to the house. Now I realise, only when you are alone, trying to hold the door closed behind you, stopping the outside from coming in.

The old man I killed comes into my head. Like Lacey, dragging himself up, step by step, turning towards me his terrified face like a lupin in a field following the sunlight. I think, I should not wander about another man's house. Lacey's sister is ill, so he left. Leaving grease on the stove and a tidy stack of newspapers in a room. I see him dead, like the drunk I killed.

The ashes of a fire stand in the centre of the room where once Lacey and I had sat. These squatters don't respect what they have. They could have brought the entire place down. I bring out the Bible and set it on the ashes. I find my book of matches and set the old paper alight, the last possession of the dead man. The burning is furious and smoke fills the room in a way I do not expect, but I do not try to open the window, fused shut as it is with old white paint.

The flickering light that fills the room is qualified by smoke. My lungs begin to ache. The stack of paper is on fire and more smoke issues out of it. I barely move, but lean my back against the wall. There is a heat rising within me, responding to the flames that are growing in the room. Should I beat it out with my coat?

Instead, my watery eyes close and they ache. My mouth is dry. The dry boards of the floor seem consumed by fire. I rise on the force of the flames, fuel for the monster that grows without relent.

Is this what I meant by coming here? To have the life drain from my limbs? I can see them as though they are not part me, but just another object in the room where we once sat, dead, inanimate. Behind closed eyes is the watery dark from where I see life evaporating off my skin, as simple as perspiration, black, indefinite. Ruth is part of me, looming in it, a network of movement in the corner of unseeing eyes. She carries a bleak expression across her face, the hopeless arch of her brow, something of the way she brings her hand to her face, then lets it fall. She emerges from an unlit hall. For a moment I imagine I can see through the window to the grey tree that now is burning. Then Dobie comes at me, all coaldust and engine grease. A man tries to leap off the tracks, but I feel the human thump he makes against the engine and turn my head. Why can I not see by the light of the flames, but I can feel the heat start from within me?

It has been black for as long as I can remember. Now there is nothing, but nor was there anything ever. I am part of the house, the brutal heat that throbs at its core. I have fallen into its inanimate design, a handle on a door, or a carved flourish in the woodwork of a fireplace. But the house comes down on me, as I am nothing. We are burned together from a book of matches, alight from the tinder of nothing. It has been black forever and I am part of the endless dark sea, I was never anything, but a flame, a car of burning coal travelling on rail through an incandescent night.

The Garbage Collectors

1.

Of course I have been played like a fool, treated with the respect fit for a rag doll. I am a chosen victim of a society I once tried to assimilate with, one suitable puppet among a hundred possible candidates. The 'mantle' of my position could be taken from me at any time and placed upon another's unfortunate shoulders and the bitter irony is that if this were to happen then my life really would be worth nothing... worth nothing in other's eyes as opposed to just mine. I am still unsure about which situation is ultimately the most destructive.

I am a jilted and stupid man, devastated at my waking and even more annoyed at my self-assisted lapse into weakness after having been consciously strong for so long. I would have been the first one to tell you that these days the greatest weakness is hope, the most obnoxious emotion is ambition and the most adolescent belief is that things will get better. I had known and lived it for thirty years and then in two small weeks I forgot it all and sold my life down a hole under the blinding lure of a piece of tail.

My tiny house behind me is quiet. A sick yellow light from a distant street lamp falls in between the gap in the curtain which I hold open to spy on to the road. The black outlines of Scavengers can be seen darting in and out of the shadows, unaware that they are one small discovery away from uncovering the treachery of an enemy.

2.

To this day it seems nobody is completely sure as to what actually happened. There is a belief in some sectors that a high ranking group of people or even one person had a clear idea of what direction the situation was taking although I am not so sure, my opinion keeps varying. At the very least I can't imagine everything that has happened would have been foreseen, that is too depressing and I would be out of a 'job'. And then, at other times, based more and more on what I see every day, I believe everything happening has been totally expected and the complete demise of an egalitarian society is coinciding perfectly with a preconceived plan...

Seemingly overnight the country's natural resources evaporated. Our once inexhaustible natural gas supply simply dried out. The countryside it seemed had been pillaged and desecrated of all its profitable reserves and was no longer in any way sustainable. News trickled in from across the country they were in their eleventh year of severe drought (I remember people at this time in the city walking around saying we weren't even aware they were in their first year of drought). There was simply no water left and huge tracts of land were lost forever to the ravages of salinity. There was no money left for grain, seed, trees, equipment, training. Whole herds of livestock were dying and crops were rendered useless. For many, for most, the situation in the country was now irredeemable.

Coupled with this (supposedly) rapid decline was the sudden realisation that the government had sold off most its departments and the remaining ruling government body were just a small bunch of powerless yesmen pandering to the demands of the unimaginably rich influential companies who now more or less controlled the country. All policy and legislation was geared towards these companies' financial success and progress – the interests of the individual were irrelevant, they simply didn't matter, there was no profit to be made from their concerns.

So even though these props of a sustainable society had been well and truly obliterated for a while people continued to live like nothing had changed. The media told us that nothing in the rest of the world had seemed to alter so clearly nothing could be changing here in a community that had mediocrity and casual apathetic continuity so ingrained within it the very thought of changed circumstance was inconceivable. Of course it was revealed later that the media reassurances up to and even beyond the time of fracturing was again governed and executed by the powerful few who wanted no unpleasantness or disruption to their system of profit until as late as possible. No panic was expressed or even felt in the middle to lower classes, the population of which seemed to double overnight – for one thing the employment dependency on the natural industries stretched much further into the workforce than I think even the majority of the hundreds and thousands of people who lost their jobs realised. It was like an old fashioned marble game. A layer shifted underneath an existing one revealing unexpected numerous disruptions on the layers above. Masses of people fell through the resulting gaps.

And then, the final straw was the news that filtered out slowly at first, first through rumour and whisper, before being announced one day through the media without any real fanfare or urgency. The government, it was revealed, had sold off all of its social security departments to multinational giant Sang Lee. In one day, with one handshake and one signature, all social security benefits had been terminated. Unemployment benefits, study allowance, war pensions, old age pensions, single parent pensions, sickness allowance – all, everything, gone, terminated. If we did not know it then we soon would – our lives had changed forever.

For the first few days no one really believed it. They continued to arrive at their local social security offices for their fortnightly payments to find them closed, locked and empty. Even then it seemed unlikely that this was happening. Soon after people remained outside waiting for them to reopen. Crowds gathered. People who had been working in the offices a week before also joined the crowd that were now in some places stretching back a hundred deep. Soon people at the back wanted to know what the hell was happening up the front so they began to make their way there to see for themselves. Old timers were roughly pushed aside, people were jostled and rolled, the fear of children began to rub off on their mothers. Tension mounted, voices rose and the crush intensified until those at the very front couldn't breath. Then a shout of terror or a snapping of sound pushed the already fragile atmosphere over the edge and the fight was on as one. The first in line suddenly discovered their misfortune as they were pierced through with splintering doors and windows as the front of the buildings exploded with the force confronting them. The disabled were trampled, children were lost and faces were torn. The fear had broken through and the biting hunger in normally well fed bellies controlled mind and action.

The shock of the now sudden desperation among the crowd hit home as disbelief turned into fury. First shops, then homes were ransacked, pubs were looted and grocery stores demolished. Shop owners who had in a day of terror lost everything joined the riots, unaware that they had already lost everything. Some shop owners did not give up their wares so easily but the sheer weight of numbers always eventually proved too strong, though not always before shots were fired. Customers who a week before were ambling down to buy some milk and bread were now being murdered by terrified proprietors. Anger fed on fear and vice versa – the fracturing had begun.

It was only when the mob approached the city and the more affluent suburbs towards the sea did a sudden knowledge of those in power reveal itself. First shots were fired into the air. Those at the front of the riots were momentarily halted but the momentum from behind was too strong and the throng of people flowed on and forward. It was only when the first advancing lines fell, pierced through with bullets, and probably more importantly when those directly behind them were sprayed with a curtain of blood from the fallen did the panic spread and the mob lose direction. A wave of hysteria and terror swept through the crowd. Any of the confused irate few who tried to slip through the line of well-armed well-guarded police were either swiftly incarcerated or, in the more dangerous cases, publicly executed.

Although this was some time ago now the metallic bite and the unexpected ferocity of those early days still echo loudly in the very uneasy balance of the present day. The society we have now is based on supervision and control or, in another way, the controlled and the controllers. There is the affluent and the powerful, still living in their houses and their communities near the city, still experiencing life very much as before. There is the city of course, the place of business and decision making, very well guarded and secure. Then there is a band of housing surrounding the inner sanctum that is populated by the lucky few who slipped through the net of bankruptcy and starvation and who now serve the upper echelon of the remaining society. This is where I now live, just lucky enough to grab a lifeline before the sickening plummet. We are a strange lot in this intermediate ground, accusing as quietly as we can the ruling class who also incidentally happen to be our only life line to an existence with some comfort. We are made up of bakers and cleaners, lower ranked policemen and tradesmen. We are completely expendable, there are literally thousands of others waiting to step into our shoes if we (for whatever reason) step aside so we must work hard and show no outward sign of disappointment or frustration. We are paid enough to live but never enough to hope, we must be content with our lot and never, never question authority.

And then finally, and most remarkably, further out, way out, almost as a clear arc miles from the centre of the city, is The Perimeter. Behind this well guarded well-monitored line is where the countless numbers of unemployed and usurped spent their days now, fighting amongst themselves for daily survival. It is a barren, dry empty landscape that these forgotten people inhabit, overpopulated and undernourished. Death and rape and filth are common themes of existence here, any manner of atrocity necessary to survive. It would be cause for international retaliation if not for two reasons. One, the international situation was not in much better shape and individual countries had enough on their own plate to deal with and two, certain government initiatives were designed to show the world the internal refugees had not been totally forgotten... and this is where the Garbage Collectors came in.

In the early days, before The Perimeter had been established, the discarded incomeless would naturally do anything to survive and, resorting to inherent animalistic traits, very quickly became the professional scavengers of society. Garbage was ransacked and pilfered to its end, anything left in the open was considered fair game. Numbers were high and competition was fierce, there was not enough garbage being generated to supply the needy. Then reports of extreme and then more common cases began filtering through. Garbage trucks had been set upon by scavenging hordes. Drivers and operators had been murdered, vehicles burnt. Steps clearly needed to be taken, boundaries established.

So the government came up with a 'solution'. The Perimeter was created. Now at random times small, supervised groups of the unemployed are allowed through The Perimeter (there is a suffocating crush each time an opportunity is announced at sets of dividing gates – the weak miss out and continue to weaken and the able fight so desperately to be included often irreparable damage is caused to the ones who are left behind). These small groups are then allowed to follow at a safe distance the garbage trucks on their weekly route. They wait patiently for any scraps thrown down to them from the Garbage Collectors. The Garbage Collectors can distribute the waste any way they see fit. They have been given the authority and the training to shoot on sight any refugee straying from the allowed path, even outside their own working hours. The Collectors are now a rank of sort in society, their position is an important and a sort after one. They are the police of the stragglers, their mood on any given day can see a family eat for a week or starve away to death.

This is the delicate balance I talk of. Murders are frequent, the affluent pay the Collectors well to keep their streets safe for themselves and their children (so far I have heard of only two cases of over-zealous Collectors mistaking a Regular for a Scavenger and only realising their error after having shot them). Now it is a common experience to be at home listening to the radio then hearing the familiar hiss and grind of a garbage truck as it goes past to be followed a few seconds later by the weak shuffle on the ground by a pack of tired hungry legs. Collections are regular and you plan your day around them – you don't want to be outside on the day of your area's collection. There is of course the protection of the Collectors but you never know, especially seeing as just recently the number of Scavengers seem to be increasing slightly.

When the situation was as bad as this it was hard to imagine it could get worse. But again for some reason unknown even to myself I was too accepting and trusting of this warped balance, too unimaginative to think this situation may not be acceptable to some. I had grown up in an apathy of acceptance and it was hard to break the habit.

3.

By some ridiculous chance of fate and while everyone else fell around me I managed to grab on to the net at the last possible moment. Six months before the announcement of the government's privitisation of Social Security I had landed the job of Assistant to the Head Greenkeeper at The Royal Botanical Gardens and Parklands. It was a large area just southwest of the city, overlooking the bay and the docklands. The only other assistants that had been working at the gardens were two old men who were employed there part-time. Unfortunately at this time age and half-measures were of no importance. I arrived at work one morning after the initial riots and they were simply not there. No mention was ever made of them, they may as well never have existed…

I was lucky enough to be kept on for two reasons. The first being that the Head Greenkeeper liked me. He was a middle-aged man with faded orange curls and broad shoulders. His name was Peter McFarlane, everyone called him Mac. He had been working at the gardens and parklands for as long as anyone could remember, or at least as long as those who mattered could remember. Like myself, he too had lost his parents in the recent turmoil but he had also lost a brother and a nephew, a great segment of his life ripped away overnight (I say 'lost' in a completely literal sense – they may have well as vanished off the face of the earth, attempts at contact between missing family members was not encouraged). Mac had a wife and three children to support so any question of him helping support his relatives was unfortunately impossible. Mac worked very hard at his job, as did I – he was constantly afraid that at any moment he and his family would be relegated to the staring masses at the edge of established society.

The second reason was simply because they needed the help (although two people was the absolute bare minimum possible to attend to the upkeep of the grounds). Given the area's size, natural quality and most importantly location it was regularly used for large government and private functions. Those who organised the events wanted everything in the best possible condition so Mac and I were constantly working, succumbing to the organiser's wishes even if their understanding of landscape usage and care was minimal. These were important occassions for the companies or whoever arranged them. Often there would be international guests visiting and they needed to be shown that the country was still a worthwhile, safe and profitable place for them to invest in. No groups of Scavengers were allowed anywhere near the gardens and parklands on the days these functions occurred. No expense was spared, no decoration too lavish and no amount of work enough – impressions had to be made.

I remember it was in the set up for one of these events that she first entered my life, I remember her very well now, a devil in angel's clothing. The event was being held by the BJK Corporation, a national multi-media company that had recently jumped a few levels to become one of the nation's strongest organisations, if not the strongest. This was an event to thank investors, shareholders and 'sympathetic' government officials for their continued support of the company.

It was proving to be one of the biggest events held at the parklands, at least during my time there. I was supervising the installation of a massive white marquee down in the lower half of the grounds, just to the left of

Bluesbry Lake, a small artificial lake full of lilies and eels. The marquee was to be used as the dancing tent and, as always on these occasions, I had the pleasure of watching the few stupid workman left in society trample over shrubs and ferns I had been nurturing for months. Ignorant bastards. Still, I was in no position to say anything. 'We do as we're told', Mac says, 'the more they destroy the more work there is for us.'

So we were just about to raise the centre pole of the marquee when around the corner from me a young woman in a red skirt and jacket holding a clipboard swung into view with Mac stumbling along beside trying to keep up with her. She was instantly beautiful, it was an obvious thing. Her blonde straight hair fell to just below her shoulders while long limbs extended gracefully out from a slim body. A black low cut blouse revealed stretches of white smooth skin and the whole effect ultimately, in my mind, was impossible. It was almost painful to see her given the complete lack of chance I would have with her given my position and occupation. She seemed to have some rank as well for as she and Mac passed me I heard her insisting that the marquee was in the wrong spot and that it should be placed on the other side of the lake. Although Mac was disputing this to a degree he was beginning to look unsure, wanting to show diligence but wary of what a mistake may mean for him.

'Look', I heard her say as they passed, showing Mac the clipboard, 'look at this design here.'

After a few more exchanged hand signals it was decided that she was right and Mac became suddenly very loud and brisk telling us to move our lazy arses and get the marquee over to the right side of the lake. Mac shot a concerned look over at me – it seemed that this was a woman you did not want to make a mistake in front of.

She stood for a while longer watching proceedings casually, very assured and content within herself. She suddenly caught me staring at her with what I can only imagine was at best a moronic face. I quickly looked away and busied myself with my work. When I shot a quick glance in her direction again she was still looking at me but now with a peculiar look on her face I couldn't decipher. I expected the poor woman was probably used to low life workers like me drooling over her. I carried on with my work and tried not to think about it.

I always wonder now whether all the resulting events from here were my fault because of my initial infatuation and at my lowest points (of which there are many) I often believe they were. I often think 'If only I hadn't looked and brought myself to her attention…' Still it is a high price to pay for a casual masculine glance at a beautiful figure, though I know now she saw it as opening, that chance moment when she dived in with heels sharpened and true intentions shrouded.

4.

Mac had left the running and cultivation of the observatory mostly in my hands. I took pride in the place and worked hard to keep it an attractive and appealing pocket of the gardens for people to visit. It was a good place to work; I enjoyed spending time in the musty earthen smell of the enclosure, the warm dampness that filled the air and the spaces between your clothes and skin. The observatory was a glass pyramid with a walkway through it that rose from the ground up to two stories high and then back again. We displayed a wide variety of exotic to the more common type of plant from the Blue Spider Orchid right through to Morning Glory.

It was around a week after the successful BJK event and I was approaching a platform on the second floor to attend to a gigantic buffalo horn we were growing there. I stopped short upon making the final turn because directly underneath admiring the plant stood the blonde haired woman from the company. A trickle of dirty water dribbled out of the spout of the watering can I was holding and splashed on to the steel railings.

'Oh, hello', she said, turning, confident, relaxed. She could afford to be. I wondered if there was someone she knew coming up behind me because it seemed unlikely that she would talk to one so obviously beneath her. I was wearing my dirty work overalls and she was immaculately dressed in a slim fitting grey dress. I turned around to see who she was talking to.

'This thing is… huge!' she continued, waving her arms around the sides of the buffalo. 'And so healthy looking. I just have to look at a plant and it dies. How do you do it?' She seemed genuinely interested, and I must admit I was very proud of the buffalo, I had rescued it from near death when I first arrived.

'You're the green keeper here, right?' she said, turning to me, her face clear in the humidity. Her eyes burned into my head. I guessed she was in her late twenties. I told her I was the assistant green keeper.

'But the observatory is your place, yes?'

I said it was. I didn't even think until much later as to why she knew this, as to why in fact she should give a fuck at all to who I was – she had me trapped and flattered in the first minute I knew her.

'Well I love this place. You've done a great job. This is by far my favourite place in the whole park.' I had never once seen her in the observatory before but what was I to do? Question the word of a beautiful woman? I found out later she had discovered a lot about me from a seemingly casual conversation with Mac two days before. She was a professional and I was a worm but from the start she treated me like an equal.

She walked towards me with her hand extended.

'Caroline Jackson.'

I took it and held her hand in mine, a smooth hand that smelled of freshly formed roses.

'Troy Brooker.'

'Well Mr Brooker' she said, angling her head to emphasise the depth of her incredible eyes, 'being the expert and all maybe you should take me a personally guided tour.'

What can I say about that afternoon? It was like I was a normal man again and we were living in a normal world. We strolled together through the gardens accompanied by a warm and open sky. I named particular plants and flowers, talked about them, talked more to a woman in this manner than I had in years. She seemed genuinely interested and relaxed but she in fact was a great actor and this was all just part of the job. Towards the end of the 'tour' she casually slipped her arm through mine. I stumbled slightly over what I had been saying and looked at her. She looked coyly back up at me, like what she had done was at great personal risk, a first daring step into unknown territory. In this one simple gesture feelings swept through me that I had never felt before and which left me as bare and open as a child. Easy prey.

At the end of that almost incomprehensible afternoon she asked me around to her house for dinner the following evening. She left me with a light brush of the fingers and a stolen kiss on the cheek. I had answered even before I knew I had spoken.

5.

I don't want to reflect too much on that first night. I am still too close to it, still too amazed about how much pleasure can bring so much ruin. Her house was larger than I could have imagined – I had no experience of such things and was so far out of my league I can see in some way she may have twisted a perverse pleasure out of me. I imagine now I am a hilarious dinner time conversation. The house was one suburb southeast of the city and my northern flat would have fit into the front room alone four times. I had dressed as best I could but still looked and felt awkward and out of place which of course she must have been prepared for. She met me at the front door full of colour and levity, a low cut green dress that revealed impossible curves of snow-white breasts. Another kiss on the cheek at welcome and then a quick tour of the ground floor (she showed me a few house ferns she told me she had been growing, probably brought in for the night) until she led me into a deep red room with it's own bar that looked out over the bay. A few thick blonde candles held pockets of light in the corners of the room. She got a stiff scotch into me as quickly as possible. After my initial revulsion and amazement at such grandeur I was soon lulled by the lush colours, the spectacular view and the smooth willing presence of Caroline.

It is painstakingly clear to me now how much of a problem the situation is to the people in control because Christ only knows how much Caroline was getting paid for her part or perhaps how much she herself had at stake. I guess I am not an ugly man but I am also very aware that I am not a 'catch', a fact made very clear to me even before the upheavals. Thick, bristly stubble sprouts in patches on my face, I have broken my nose twice and I am already balding quite dramatically. So who knows apart from Caroline herself what she was thinking when later that night, after more drink and a number of delicate, seemingly casual contacts, she took the glass from my hand and placed her full long lips over the stretch of mine and then continued down the rigid length of my body to a part that had not been visited by anyone but myself for a very long time. Her sweet blonde hair fell around my lap as her lips sunk over the shaft of my prick and drew back as slow as the night itself. In the moments before I came I was in a haze of unexplored lands, blissfully unaware that all of my life and all of my future was gently being swallowed away.

6.

The next two weeks (she only needed two weeks – I imagine now she was counting down the days) sting me as deeply now as much as they swept me away then. I was often at her house (she understandably never came to mine) – we had dinners together, slept together, she even brought me a picnic lunch to work one day. She told me she was a freelance events director to major investment companies and that she was having a wonderful time with me. If things had lasted any longer then perhaps I would have asked her about her motives (I was a lowly paid labourer with no chance of real improvement) but as they were I was blinded with skin and sex and mansions and expensive alcohol. I was happy, and any taste of that emotion for a man like me these days is more than enough to turn you into a malleable, stumbling lap dog.

Only once did I have a chance to glimpse under the fabric, to spot the underlying web of deceit that surrounded me. Caroline and I were walking together past the brown river that runs through the middle of the city when we came across a group of three older businessmen deep in discussion. One of them, a thickset man wearing a red tie and with thin sandy hair, looked up and saw us. He continued to stare at us. Caroline, who had been looking out over river, glanced back and saw this man watching. She slid her arm out of mine and took a quick step in front of me.

'You keep walking', she said directly, quietly, 'okay, you just keep walking.'

I was going to say something but she hissed 'Just do it.' I wasn't too worried, I imagined it was a work colleague and it wouldn't be in Caroline's best interest to be seen with me. I kept walking along the river, past the men and further on.

When I looked back Caroline was facing the other way talking to the men who were all angled so as they could see me. They diverted their attention back to Caroline when I turned around. They all exchanged a few more quiet words then Caroline moved away from the group and skipped on over to me with her long slim legs. She took my arm in her hand and moved us on.

'I thought I told you to keep on walking', she said brightly, nudging into me a little.

'Who were those guys? Was it okay you being seen with me?'

'Oh of course, they were just some old work friends.'

I said I knew, that's what I had thought.

'Good, good for you. You understand me not introducing you though, don't you?'

'Yes, of course. God yes.'

'Good. But oh, I don't know, because of that maybe you should come back to my house and we can, you know, maybe fool around a bit.'

Again the coy, innocent look up at me from those intensely feminine eyes. I told her she was amazing, I let her know how I felt. She giggled and nudged into me closer, the smell of her immaculate hair coming up and out at me.

I was amazed at the way things were going. I had no thoughts or illusions about the future, no concerns or expectations for even the next day. I was spending time with a beautiful woman, I was having *sex* with a beautiful woman, I was feeling good about myself and for a time nothing else mattered. So when Caroline rang one evening and organised to meet me the next day for coffee all I was thinking about was how long it would be before I would again be watching the white canvas of her body being unsheathed in the middle of the deep, warm night.

7.

We had arranged to meet at midday in a little café unknown to me at the west end of the city. This was an unpopular area for most of the affluent. The west end angled round into the cities vast industrial docklands. Although the docklands were still necessarily operational they offered the least amount of protection and security from trespassing vagrants – the docklands covered such a vast area there were plenty of unguarded holes the desperate could slip through. It was a strange in-between space but still I didn't think too much of Caroline's request to meet there, she hadn't shown any great similarities with the severely affluent anyway – one look at me would tell you that.

The café was at the far end of a main city street, just up from the abandoned state train station. It was a Sunday so a normally populated street had turned into a wasteland. City noises came in from a distance while empty plastic soft drink bottles rolled down the street and into the sun. Empty parts of the city like this always unnerved me even in the normal times – today the heat and the lack of breeze added to the desolation of the scene. The café itself had a brown façade and across the front doorway an old fly proof curtain stretched its thin plastic fingers downward to the floor. A noisy air-conditioner blasted down at the top of your head as you entered.

There was only one other person inside the café besides Caroline, a wrinkled old woman wearing wide sunglasses motionless at a back table. Caroline herself had on a pair of thin-framed reading glasses I had not seen before and was wearing a grey sleeveless top with grey slacks – very official and business like for a weekend I thought. A black briefcase sat waiting on the floor beside her.

I wandered over to her and made to give her a kiss on the cheek. She fended me off.

'Take a seat please', she said stiffly.

I did. The plastic chair dragged along the dirty green floor.

'What's up?'

Caroline reached down to her briefcase and produced a file. She placed it on the table in front of her.

'Take a look at these.'

She passed me a collection of photographs. I looked at the first few and felt they were innocent enough. There were a couple of shots of me at work, black and white, planting shrubs and watering. The next was of me entering my local supermarket. The next entering my house. I didn't understand the significance of the photographs at all. I didn't know why they existed, how Caroline had obtained them and why she was showing them to me.

The next photograph was one of me cooking inside my kitchen. I felt a strange sudden itch underneath my collar. Caroline watched me impassively. In the background the old woman with the dark sunglasses continued to look straight ahead. Unfortunately I flipped over to final photograph. It was a clear shot of me sitting in my tiny front room masturbating.

'Oh, Caroline, I – '

'And take a quick look at this.'

She passed me a thin sheaf of paper. I scanned lightly down the page. My address, my bank account number, my bank balance, my PIN number, my tax file number, a copy of my last pay slip, a copy (for Christs sake) of my last shopping docket, my employment history, my education history, the registration of the last car I owned…anything and everything that in some way related to my life. I felt mystified, unhitched.

Caroline took the documents and the photographs back and placed them in the folder. She held the folder up.

'This – you see this Troy? This is your life, all of it. I have all of your insignificant little life in my hands.'

I was too stupefied to really comprehend this dramatic change of attitude within Caroline since I had last seen her – none of her charm and appeal were on show this time. She continued.

'I have told you what I do but that is really only part of my job. The other part of my occupation is much larger and really much more important than the piddling little events I organise. I am a key representative for a recently formed organisation called The Assembled League of Producers and, through me, I am glad to inform you that you have been lucky enough to be chosen to be included in their employ.'

These are the words she used – 'lucky enough to be chosen'. They must laugh like hell about this somewhere.

'Let me set out your new job for you. You will earn twenty dollars for each completed task and in the beginning there may be up to four tasks a week. It will interfere with your present job, arrangements have already been made. If you do not comply with any of the specifications I introduce you to today, well we will simply throw your life away.'

I looked at her looking at me. Her face showed no emotion – she was clearly just doing her job. The two rides of our recent experience together were only now becoming one. I felt unusually hot and more confused than if I were a child.

'The unemployed are beginning to become a major problem – are you listening?' I hadn't been. I was trying to fathom some semblance of dignity but it was proving more difficult than I could manage.

'Pay attention. The numbers of unemployed and homeless are beginning to become a major problem. There are simply too many of them and far too many of them are slipping through into established areas and causing disturbances. They are naturally very desperate and more and more are prepared to thieve and destroy anything that aids their hope for survival. This is beginning to make the people I represent very uneasy.'

'How sad for them', I mumbled.

'I beg your pardon? I don't need to remind you who you are working for now do I?'

Her voice planted a taste in my mouth like bitter steel, she narrowed her eyes and looked like someone I had never seen before.

'Of course we cannot have a massive cull of these people, it would unfortunately damage essential ties with other more secure countries, so I'm afraid the method we adopt must be of a more subtle nature.'

She reached down to the briefcase.

'This is now your new mobile phone. It can only receive calls, you cannot make any yourself – '

'Caroline, Caroline', I said abruptly. 'This… I mean you're joking right? What about – '

'Us? I knew you were right for this job, such levels of naivety are essential – do you really think my name is Caroline?'

She had blinded me with breasts and lies and naked showers in the mornings – I had stumbled on behind like a plaything.

'Now shut up and listen. You must keep this mobile phone on and charged at all times. I don't need to stress the importance of this and the ramifications of what will happen if you don't, do I? Good. When you are called you will be given an address and a location. You will also be given a car – a car and a phone, quite the fringe benefits aren't they? The car will be monitored at all times so before any thoughts begin to gather in your grubby little mind just realise there is nowhere you can go without us knowing about it. Now, when you drive to the specified location there will be at least one package for you to pick up. After this you will drive home and place the package or packages, whatever the case may be, into your rubbish bin, and that is your part of the deal done okay? Easy.'

It was clear the term package was a commonly used phrase in this new world I was being exposed to. Anyway, my understanding of the term sounded like it would be confirmed soon enough.

'Any failure to comply with these instructions will have immediate and devastating effects for you. The Garbage Collectors have your name and address and will also be supplied with the information of how many packages you are expected to have in your rubbish bin each week, so any discrepancy with their information and the actual contents will instantly be known and will effectively be dealt with. Do you understand?'

I said nothing. I continued looking at the table in front of me.

'Are there any questions?'

'They'll figure it out soon enough,' I said in a low voice, 'when they realise no-one is returning. Then they'll stop coming through the Perimeter into the established areas and there won't be any need for me.'

She laughed a little and leaned back on her chair.

'You obviously don't understand the enormity of this problem. If they stop coming through then we'll go looking for them, see? This is a major problem for industry that needs to be handled very delicately. Things must seem to be as normal as possible but those beyond the Perimeter and the like are a major drain on resources, funds, not to mention the quality of living for those that deserve it…'

'You must be joking,' I spat, 'for those that deserve it!'

'Listen,' she said, suddenly leaning forward, 'don't fuck with me. I am not a person to be fucked with. It is your life and you can throw it away if you like, I really don't care, you must understand this. There are plenty of other guys dicks I can suck to make this happen so don't begin to think your special or something, but be assured, Bruce, or whatever your fuck-ugly name is, your services will be required as long as you can supply them.'

She stood and pushed her chair under the table.

'Your car is the white sedan outside, here are the keys. You life will be not that greatly different – I'm sure you'll find a way to live with it, but as I say, that choice is yours. If you are seen on the grounds of my house you will be shot.'

And with that the woman I had known as Caroline left the café walking briskly on the balls of her feet. I stayed sitting at the shitty little table in the café for almost an hour, too stunned to move. I found the car outside and drove off down the street in a world that to me looked very different from a few hours ago.

8.

A call has come through. It is the fifth already this week and it is only Thursday. The location of the pick up is not that far from where I live and this has been an increasing trend over the last couple of weeks. Most of the work in the first three or four months was closer into the city and nearer the richer suburbs as the woman (Caroline) said it would be but more recently I have had to pick up the murdered bodies of the unemployed further out in more second rate suburbs like my own. I feel I carry no emotion with my new employment but I also feel somewhere beneath me something is knotting like a fury of the blood.

All the money I earn for my work I spend on alcohol. It sometimes contains raging panics in the night if and when I have fallen asleep. I had been expecting it to happen but not so quickly. On the outskirts of the docks two weeks into my collecting I was picking up the green garbage bag that held another murdered unfortunate and the man's head lolled out the top of the bag, his neck punctured with bullet holes. I looked at the wide silent eyes and the strands of neck still connecting his head to the rest of his body and recognised him as an old school friend of mine, Paul…

I don't know, my thoughts are everywhere. Recently at a pub I saw another man with exactly the same car as mine and the same look of distance and disbelief I have noticed etching its way on to my face. We didn't talk but I realised then there was more than one of us. This made me feel better for an instant, but only for an instant.

The unemployed are not stupid and they know they are disappearing and yet they have no avenue of release for their frustration and anger. Monday nights are my bin nights but I wait for as long as possible now before I put it out – what incentives would there be if the contents of my bin were to be discovered by Scavengers who continue to hunt the streets? There would be no Garbage Collectors to protect me until the morning anyway… There cannot be too many solutions now. I doubt I can continue, I may see what three packets of Panadeine and half a cartoon of beer can do, I don't know, I don't know…

I expect somebody somewhere is happy, or is still aware as to what feelings that concept pertains to. For myself, strands of dying flesh I think are beginning to pervade my house and smell very much to me like the stupidity of our times.

Dark Rooms of Light (Variations)

Anonymity (1)

Charlie slowed the car down at the gate to show the bloke his stolen tip pass, and then followed the signs to where the newest mountain of refuse was as tall as the nearest eucalypt. Mick sat next to him with the paper open in his lap, but talked all the way regardless. Charlie pulled up near the rubbish, but didn't bother to back the trailer in.

'It fuckin' stinks,' said Mick, folding his paper, not wanting to get out of the car before Charlie did.

'You talk too much, mate,' said Charlie.

The dirt road had been blackened by oil and when they put their feet out on to it, their heels sunk in, because the rain had turned it to mud. Mick hitched the legs of his pants and pulled up his socks.

'I'm goin' for a wander,' he said. 'Unload it yerself.'

Charlie opened the boot and found the shovel before leaping into the trailer. He stared at the pale soil he was about to toss; it had rearranged itself on the drive, formed patterns and ridges like beach sand caught beneath the swell. If you stare at it long enough, he thought, it begins to shimmer, so it took a while before he drove the shovel into the illusion, ruining everything. As he looked down into the deception of the sand, he thought about how nothing was really as it appeared. Finally, he heaved a full shovel forward, over the side of the trailer, straining beneath the weight of it.

Gulls followed Mick everywhere he went. They formed a single file behind him that he occasionally turned to and swung his arms at, scattering birds away from him. He could hear Charlie grunting with each hoist of the shovel.

As he looked around the dump, it seemed to Mick that all the debris and detritus could not really be unwanted. He wondered if the parts of the world you found at the tip had been left in the weather by accident. Smashed up radios, bald tyres, bed springs, bicycle spokes, the innards of a generator. All of it still had purpose. Every piece was an artefact still valuable to anyone who cared enough to think about it. He could have spent hours cataloguing the lot, but loved to see it strewn in the mud, wet and abandoned. He imagined he understood the terrible beauty in the sadness of it all, the way you saw an old chair standing aside from the other wreckage, the leather torn off it and the springs hanging out. He liked to say that every orphan once had parents.

He kicked at the piles with his boots, overturning them, trying to see what was underneath. The nervousness of the gulls unsettled him, so he struggled over an impressive embankment to where the dump met the bush and rummaged through as much refuse as he could bear to smell. He went over to a corrugated iron sheet, kicked off the broken crates that covered it and lifted it clear. A suitcase was half buried in the damp soil, an old one, built solidly and lined with dark, damp leather. Mick reached down and heaved it from the earth, falling backwards on his arse as it came free.

Instead of opening it, he carried it back to Charlie, who had finished the unloading and was sitting on the car, kicking at the tyre with his heels.

'What's that, mate?' asked Charlie.

'Old suitcase. Found it behind that huge hill of shit.' He pointed with his thumb.

'What's in it?' Charlie slid off the car.

'Dunno.'

Mick tossed the old suitcase on the ground and they both craned their necks to make sure that the bloke who checked the tip passes wasn't around. Charlie found a hammer under the back seat and smashed off the locks.

'Once I found ten years worth of daily papers,' said Mick. 'The old boy who bought them never had the time to read them all and couldn't stomach chucking them out. He was a mate of a mate. The wife finally chucked them when he died. You know that clipping I got on the fridge of me presenting the fairest and best? That's where it's from. December 4, 1972.'

They lifted the lid of the suitcase and found hundreds of photographs, maybe more than a thousand. Some were old, some were in colour. They picked them up by the handful and could see that no one person was in more than a couple of shots; they had found someone's collection of strangers. Family photographs, formal portraits and several sketches spilled over the sides of the suitcase. Mick found a series that looked as though they had been taken on a busy street; taken without the knowledge of their subjects, as though these strangers were just walking past, captured in a moment of absence. They adjusted hats or looked thoughtlessly at their feet. In one, a drunk held his head in his hands, almost with grief, perhaps regretting his inebriated self. In another, an old woman laughed, holding her head back. You could just glimpse a young woman (her daughter?) walking beside her. Some of the photographs had writing scrawled in the margins or on the back.

Charlie found a photograph of a woman. It was larger than the rest. She was looking up into the camera, wrapped in a sheet and a blanket, her blonde hair dark in the black and white. He stared at it a long time before showing Mick, who shrugged it off. Charlie held it up to the light and turned it in his fingers. On the back, someone had written in pencil, 'To you who will soon disappear, from she who remains.' He could almost let himself believe that he knew her; the empty eyes and the luniform mouth seemed almost familiar. Who captured her at that instant? Her image in paper seemed to Charlie something that was greater than any person; as if all that was left of her was the way she had reflected light at that moment. As if the illusion of her memory was greater than the reality of what she had once been.

Mick slammed the suitcase shut and Charlie was left holding the photograph of the woman. It made him nervous because he didn't know what to do with it, except that he wanted to keep holding it.

'Maybe someone didn't mean to throw them out,' said Mick, who had lifted the suitcase and heaved it into the back seat.

'What should we do with it?'

'Get it home, go through it, then try to sell it. If we can't, we'll give it back.'

'Maybe we should keep it?'

Mick screwed up his face. 'Waste of space.'

Without realising it, Charlie was again examining the photograph of the woman, bringing it close to his eyes. He studied the space and light. Then her expression, her parted lips. She who remains. He could not even guess how old it might have been. She who remains ageless, caught in the aspect of chemical light, as if it was the woman herself who had been burned on the paper.

They hurried into the car because they could see the ticket inspector coming over. Charlie let his photograph rest on the dashboard.

But it didn't matter how old the woman had become. Charlie realised, as he drove out of the tip, that she was only a note in the margin. All there could have ever been was the camera, releasing its mechanism, receiving whatever light radiated from the bulb, lingering on the chemistry of the paper.

Everything was the photograph, sliding along the dashboard like something he could easily forget.

'There's something about this one,' said Mick, picking it up with his outstretched arm, holding like he didn't have his glasses on. 'I had a photo like this of Elly. You know how she hates her photo taken. Real bloody struggle. But once she gave in, it was the biggest smile you'd ever seen. Shame, but we lost it. God knows where it went.'

'Maybe it got chucked out,' Charlie said. He thought about it and grinned.

'God knows. Disappeared into thin air, I suppose.'

The bloke who checked the tip passes stood by the chicken wire fence and watched them disappear behind the road works.

Enmity

The grey hair that she couldn't arrest in her ponytail was cleaved forward on her forehead and her temples. She stooped on the corner near the town hall, looking up at strangers who hurried passed as she tried to catch an eye, as if she had something intimate to murmur into an half turned ear. If you moved past her too slowly she would try and stuff a handful of photographs into your coat, shoving out her open hand for money.

Orson saw her and thought about crossing to the other side of the road. The light rain that had been falling had stopped and sunlight appeared in a reassuring column of heat. He had finished work, loosened his necktie and walked the long way from the office to the bus stop. He decided to pass her, feeling the pinprick of curiosity.

'How much for a handful of memories, Mister?' She lunged at him, thrusting forward the photographs. 'This is all I got, a few photos of the kids. Must be worth five at least for all I got left.'

'Five dollars for these?' he looked at them, pictures of children with sallow eyes. He counted three boys and a girl. 'I'll give you two.'

'C'mon mate, I'm above begging. I'm selling everything I have left. It's the only way I'll eat tonight, if someone's gonna buy these.'

'What about your kids?'

She gripped his arms and pulled herself close, so he could smell the tobacco smoke in her hair. 'They're dead, mate. Killed by their fuckin' old man. Gassed 'em in the car. You have to buy 'em. They're the world me, so they gotta be worth something to you.'

He fished through his pockets until he found the last of his gold coins and counted them out into her hand. She stared at the photograph for a moment before opening his coat to find a pocket, looking up at him. There was nothing in her eyes, as if she was blind or beyond grief.

'Keep them,' he said, trying to force them back to her, but she threw up her hands, and then covered her face with them. As she turned from him, Orson hurried away, thinking how badly she'd been humiliated. The photographs had become creased in his hand. He stopped and rested his back against a stone wall, examining them. Four children with blond hair, stiff with portraiture, staring sightlessly into the lens. She had been desperate to sell them, to prove she was not a beggar. But how could he keep them? He thought perhaps she had purchased her dignity with his guilt. He almost tore them up and tossed them into the rain water that pooled at his feet. They could have been snatched from the mantle of any house, children with combed hair and straightened collars, a mother with a moistened handkerchief demanding grins so wide they became ghoulish.

'What about the woman,' he thought, so he retook his steps, quicker than he had taken them in the first place. The woman hadn't gone. She stood thrusting another handful of photographs at a stranger. Orson stopped to watch her.

'How much for all I've got?'

'What have you got?' A young man had stopped to answer her.

'Pictures of my husband. All I got left of him after he died of cancer.'

The young man took the photographs to examine them before searching his pockets for money.

Orson bit his lip and waited until the young man found his wallet before hurrying to the woman. She looked at him with the same desolate eyes.

'Keep your money, mate,' he said. 'It's all bullshit.' He took the photographs she was about to sell to the young man. In them a man with glasses and a beard held up a brace of fish for the camera, his arms raised almost wearily, as if he regretted catching them at all.

'I thought he killed himself,' Orson shouted at the woman. She covered her face with her hands, like she was an animal anticipating a blow. The young man turned and hurried away, more from Orson than from the woman. Orson threw the photographs at her and they landed at her feet. She scurried away, almost running, but Orson didn't follow. He felt the muscles in his legs solidify, felt the angles and the lines of the street converge on him.

He tried to make sense of it as he watched her disappear. The fiction of her tragedy had become real as she scurried away as best she could. It was as though the photographs were the abstraction of what she had become, the corporeal flesh and blood of a woman closer to fraud than to charity. He kicked the wall so hard he thought he broke his foot.

Rain began to fall again, so there was nothing for him to do but pick up the photographs and hurry away. He took another look before tossing them into the bin.

He wished he knew the people whose images he discarded. Had she stolen the pictures? Four children and the man with the beard, each of them so different to the woman who had tried to sell them. He could have laughed at himself, a ridiculous figure, half alive in the mounting drum of the downpour. He listened to it hit his shoulders with its fatness.

Turning once more for the bus stop and trying to forget himself, he muttered under his breath, cursing her and flinging out his arms. He looked up into the rain, realizing that she had the last of his cash and that the bus had already gone.

Obscurity

Sunday was slow. The studio had been empty since he opened it that morning, but he sat there anyway, half asleep on a wooden chair he had moved to the centre of the room, into the column of light that sluiced the window panes. He warmed himself like a cat, his eyes half closed.

By eleven o'clock he had finished cleaning his camera for a second time and went back to sprawling in his chair. The sun prickled his skin through his woollen jumper, as if it had fingers of its own, moving over his flesh with its physical invisibility.

He leapt to his feet when the bell rang and stood gathering himself as he listened to a man coughing. He had not heard the door open because his eyes had just closed and his hands had fallen heavily by his sides. As he walked out into the reception, the man stood at the counter, regarding his own reflection in the mirror by the door.

'Are you the photographer?' he asked, still examining himself.

'Yes. Have you booked?'

'You're not really busy. Can't see a problem, can you, mate?'

The man looked up at the photographer for the first time and returned his glare. He stood with his hands in his pockets, his feet planted firmly, as if he had grown there out of the ground. They stared at each other for a moment, thinking of what to say next. The man began to look nervous.

He said: 'This might sound strange and I don't really want to go into it, but I need a photo of me without my clothes on.'

The photographer began to turn away from him. 'Sorry, mate. Can't do that. We're family photographers.'

'I'll make it worth your while.'

'We do mums and dads and kids, mate. That's it.'

The man took out his wallet and lined up ten notes on the counter. The photographer counted them, and looked up. The man stared at him, still nervous. At some point the photographer's silence became acceptance and the man thrust forward his open palm to introduce himself, a smile having stretched across his lips.

'Thanks, mate. My name's Ferguson.' As if knowing his name would make it easier.

The photographer didn't shake his hand, but instead gathered up the notes and pointed his thumb to the door of the studio. Then he followed Ferguson through it.

For a moment, the photographer contemplated the possibility he may have made a mistake and ran his hand through his oily, black hair. He went to his camera and loaded it. Ferguson stood in the part of the studio where he guessed the subject stood and put his arms out. The photographer couldn't resist raising the camera and photographing him as his mouth began to open. The studio lights flashed in expiration and Ferguson blinked.

'So what do you want me to do?' he asked.

The photographer sighed, and then said, 'Well, mate, I suppose you'd better take your clothes off, then.'

Ferguson did not believe that he could have been any more naked, with the lights holding him in their glare, and the photographer staring at him through the lens, then measuring the light around him. He began to peel away his clothes, first unbuttoning, then revealing slowly – slower as the photographer became impatient. Eventually, he was naked and stood in the light like a pale limbless stump.

The photographer thought he had diminished without his clothes, as though he had begun to shed his flesh. As though he waited to be photographed wearing only his bones. Perhaps, thought the photographer, Ferguson had become transparent, as though the light was so brilliant that it burnt through him, leaving only his ribs and a shadow on the wall. He had become clean, purified in the shine and glimmer. It could have been that he had just appeared unexpectedly from behind a curtain; you would be surprised into studying him, unnaturally pale except for a dark pubis, his arms falling uselessly at his sides.

He began with a close up of the face. Focused on his eyes, taking in the new stubble that broke through his chin. Then he stepped backwards and framed the polished limb of his body. His bare feet were fixed heavily on the floor.

'Am I right like this?' asked Ferguson, but the photographer did not reply, so he folded his arms and frowned. The light was in his eyes and he couldn't see much beyond them. He had never before been so naked, translucent in the spotlights. He felt as though every part of himself was in fine detail, as though he could see into his own pores, through his own flesh.

The photographer finished a film. 'Get your clothes back on,' he said and walked to the workbench where he unloaded the camera. Ferguson pulled on his pants and buttoned himself, finally pulling his belt tight.

'How long?' he asked. The photographer shrugged. The red light of the dark room already spilled through the door.

Ferguson stiffened, reanimated now that the lights were off and his clothes were on. 'I'll be back in an hour,' he said. 'Make sure they're ready.'

The photographer huffed as he went to the darkroom and shut the door behind him. He waited until Ferguson shut the front door as he left. Then he poured the chemicals and the air became filled with their sourness. Eventually, Ferguson's image filtered through the white of the paper. The photographer clipped an image to the line to dry and considered its subject, drowning in the brilliant red of the darkroom. His insignificant limbs became red with light.

How could I have done this? thought the photographer and hurried Ferguson through the chemical process. He paused to finger the notes he had folded in his pocket.

The photographs were pinned up carefully and he saw each of them, one at a time, in their series; a man's face balanced against the overexposed body and the dark flaw of his cock. In the next, his arms were leaving his sides as though he was about to reach forward. The photographer fell back into a chair. The man he had photographed was grotesque and unreal. He had become a pale shadow on the paper, as though everything pierced him.

He waited until the photographs dried, slid them into an envelope and went to the reception to wait for Ferguson to return. It was later in the day when he did, opening the door in a hurry and surprised to find the photographer leaning against the counter with the yellow envelope in his hands.

Ferguson said nothing, but walked across the room and took the envelope from the photographer's loose fingers. He opened it and spread the photographs over the dark wood of the counter.

'This is not it,' he said. 'This is not what I wanted at all.'

The photographer realised that Ferguson was unbalanced by what he saw. 'You wanted a portrait,' he said, speaking softly. 'These are what you asked for. You wanted your clothes off. Here it is, mate.'

'I've forgotten to smile,' said Ferguson, to which the photographer shrugged. 'You've made me look…fake. Like you can see right through me.'

The photographer had not expected him to understand what he had done and was astonished. 'It's the light. It makes you look more real, as if the focus was better.' But Ferguson was transparent, like a faded colour still clinging to old walls.

Ferguson put the photographs back in the envelope and tucked it under his arm. Without another word, he turned away and back out on to the street, pulling the door closed hard behind, so that the window panes rattled in the sills.

The studio fell silent like a bell that had finished ringing. The photographer drew a breath and saw that his warm light had passed away from the studio. Even though it was just that the day had grown longer, it was as though the man's obscene nudity had changed the aspect of the room, as if the corners had been taken off everything. Ferguson was like dirt on his hands. He burned the negatives, watching them melt in the flame he had lit in the darkroom sink.

Without even thinking about it, he moved his chair out to where the sunlight had cast itself earlier in the day.

He drew his arms around himself, almost regretting that he had destroyed the negatives. It was strange that he never asked why the man needed the photographs in the first place. He laughed, imagining them framed and hung in his hallway, perfect in their deformity. He stood and went to the door, locking it with a turn of the wrist, and then cleaned his camera again, wiping down the parts with a rag.

At that moment nothing could have extricated him from the studio and he closed his eyes to picture Ferguson standing in it naked. Next Sunday will be quiet, he thought, and I'll sleep in the sun.

Anonymity (2)

Katherine opened the local paper to find a photograph of a photograph of herself. In the floury ink, two men held it up in front of a suitcase full of old photographs. The image stirred up memories. She could not prevent the handled flesh of that day returning, the way his shirt fell open as he held the camera above her and how she was surprised he had laughed, smacking his dry lips at her stretched out limbs. Why do these things return at all? she asked herself. Time had not hardened her, as she would have thought. It was the image of herself, so familiar, but complicated by the blood that rushed to her head.

The headline read: 'Suitcase holds secrets,' and she huffed at this, lowering her face close to the page, studying the photograph she had not seen in so many years. More attractive than she remembered, especially her painted lips. She could have kissed her own mouth so much harder than he would have dared. She studied herself how he would have seen her, paused above her with a camera, light divided by the convex of a lens, the chemistry of it all.

Two men had found the collection he had only just embarked upon when she met him. He would cover a table with photographs of strangers, pointing out their peculiarities. He kept only those that he said affected him. 'The best ones change me,' he used to say. There was no order to it, only the setting of the muscles in his face and the concentration as it twitched in his eyes. She would put her fingers in the oil of her hair, trying to see what he saw, imagining the profiles of strangers that he would pin to the walls.

The memory of his apartment became real for a moment. She was again standing in the doorway, her hand on the iron knob, watching him as sleep rearranged the hairs of his moustache. Once more, she was leaving, pulling the heavy door closed quietly behind her.

Had he survived the years that they had been apart? Had he died? Why would his collection, including the photograph of her – including her – be found thrown away, in the midst of the world's refuse? Sitting at the table, her eyes fixed to the image of herself, it occurred to her that she was now exactly what he would have photographed. A woman who had forgotten herself, who was absent from everything except what she had once been.

She felt the sting of the brine swelling in her eyes, as though life had moved against her in black and white, staring up from the grub of news-print, forcing her to a crisis of tears.

In another room, her husband dragged his chair across the wooden floor and she was surprised into closing the paper. Even if he opened it, her would not recognise the soft face, thirty years younger than hers; even if he had, would she have needed to explain? It was all in the photograph, her image staring out into the flesh of her ageing face.

'Where are you, darling?' she called to him, rearranging herself like flow-ers in a vase. In case he rushed in as sometimes he did. She heard him cough, then again scrape the chair. Saved from weeping, she stood, rebal-ancing her geometry as she headed through the door to find him.

'In the kitchen,' he called, just before she saw him, seated at the table, absent hands filing through letters and advertisements. He looked up and said, 'Look at this shit. In never ends.' He turned back to it. 'It never ends, does it?'

It could have been that she had no ending, the way she looked at him, paused in the doorway, wanting to drive her hands through his hair or rest her cold palms against the flush of his throat. She felt as if she could have been made of stone; the work of masons, transfixed and immutable, the arched lines of her face incapable of expression.

He pushed his papers away and leaned into his chair, its feet again scor-ing the floorboards. The way he looked at her reminded her that she was still wet from the squall that had erupted. She had just collected the mail from the box and tossed it on to the table. Except for the paper. The rain was still dividing itself on the roof tiles.

'It's really coming down,' she said.

'Has been for days. You could have left those,' he said and passed his hand over the mail she had thrown.

'You just said it never ends. Here it is, then. Never ending.' She walked to the refrigerator, feeling the slackness in her body that she tried to make hard. Padding soles on cold tiles. How closely was he watching her? She tried to look invisible. Could he see anything but the urgency of unopened mail? This world, she thought, had become as thin as water, as if it had been passed through a sieve.

'Do you remember Berlin?' he asked. Her eyes became cold. 'The rain never stopped the entire week. And not one single fucking taxi.'

'I remember,' she said. 'We were always soaked through.'

He laughed. Another of his memories fished from the pickling jar, she thought. Then he reached for his papers again. Endless words, perpetual balancing. She kept the refrigerator door open long enough to pretend she was looking, then hurried from the room, before he could say something else.

Diminished by the refraction of her escape, she breathed deeply the air outside the kitchen. She opened the paper to find herself again, still fixed there, eyes that consumed, the suppliant mouth. For the moment, she imagined the photograph could not have been of her and thought of how quickly strangers must have passed over it: another irrelevancy in the local news. She admitted to herself that she had become embarrassed. Katherine, she reminded herself, of everything you have done with yourself, this is the least cause for shame. Think of the inflexibility of his naked flesh; the rigid, unbearable strength of his back. What would age have done to him? She smiled and thought of the running colours of an old photograph. How nothing burned so permanently on paper could be the same on different days.

And that's all it is, she thought, leaning over the page, a terrible confluence of nothing. All I will be is the chemistry of a photograph, how I changed the light for a trick. A trick of the eyes, she guessed, guessing too that the black and white of newsprint went further into the world than she ever could have. A trick of light, of the eyes.

I cannot see anything, she thought, except that which I once was.

Her husband called out to her, as if to say: 'Come and look,' but she closed her eyes, screwing the paper in her fist, so that when she opened them, the pages were mangled and torn, ink staining her pale fingers. She could explain a missing paper, but there were no words for the history she had almost forgotten. So she screwed it up into a ball and threw it across the room.

Her eyes closed again without her being aware of it.

So long ago, she thought. His face had not been as fixed as hers was. His still suspended out of reach. They had exchanged glances between the bookshelves before he leant into her in an aisle, parting her with the layers of his breath.

'I wonder if you could help me,' he had said, changing the meaning of it with the sallow of his eyes and a flex in his mouth.

Those days ran quicker than any others, as if they knew time was running out, that it was escaping from them like a handful of tossed grain. Their terrifying kisses became furious, closing over each other with their hunger. In all of this there was a weakness, because their desire was born from nothing more than the fear of absence. She brought her body to him so it would not be without longing. This is what he had photographed; how her face became flushed with emptiness, a vacancy that carried every muscle of her desire, but which was ultimately nothing other than an image for the film.

Her husband came into the room and said something.

'Sorry,' she replied. 'I was lost in thought.'

His mouth moved, words spilling out that she couldn't grasp. She thought that she could never return from so much memory. He waved his hand in front of her unseeing eyes and startled her.

'Lost in thought,' he said.

'That's one way to put it.' She felt his hands brush over her shoulders and couldn't bear it. She rushed from the room and left him to stare at her absence, that place near the door where she had once been. The frailty of his voice called after her, a flutter of wings that seemed to follow her through the door, around the corners.

What happened to that man from years ago? she thought. The one with the camera that still captured her. Had time closed him down? On a warm day in April she never went back, taking her lunch and catching the train north, accepting the absence of his skin, how his hands were missing from between her thighs. Going nowhere in the carriage of a train.

It all just happened, she thought. I hadn't planned it. It was as if she was looking back on yesterday's weather; gone, but somehow still there, almost imperceptibly.

She found her car keys beneath a stack of magazines, left the house and drove into the city. Nothing could explain this, she thought. She could not even describe it to herself. She parked near the railway station and rushed to the white booth that took passport photos. She drew the curtain closed behind her and emptied the change from her purse.

The flash went off again and again as she sat in front of the camera. Each time the machine stopped, she fumbled more coins into the slot. With each photograph, her face became more ordinary. Without expression. Almost as though she was barely alive. She held the photographs against her belly, looking down on them as the machine worked again. When she ran out of change she fell through the curtain and onto the tarmac. A cold wind had begun to blow through the station. She clutched the photographs of her naked, voiceless face in a way that made her feel more real, as if she was more than light captured on the film.

I am more than that, she thought, more than a square of paper in the fingers of strange men. She had a name. She had countless faces, spilling out of the machine.

With an effort, she picked herself up, but stumbled. The car seemed far away. What have I become? she asked herself. Where are the two men who discovered my fate, my other life on the seas of the dump? Picked up, examined, pocketed.

A gust caught her by surprise and loosened her fistful of photographs. They scattered like seed, disappeared beneath benches and over the tracks. Before she could think of the tears that welled in her eyes, she imagined that the photographs were like children. Pictures of her that were escaping, leading anonymous lives, carried away on themselves like the gearless flight of birds.

Go forth, she thought, before falling to her knees.

www.ingramcontent.com/pod-product-compliance
Lightning Source LLC
Chambersburg PA
CBHW020646250626
47154CB00008B/2824